Escape from Happytown

Tim Miller

Copyright © 2015 Tim Miller

All rights reserved. No part of this publication may be reproduced, distributed, or transmitted in any form or by any means, including photocopying, recording, or other electronic or mechanical methods, without the prior written permission of the publisher, except in the case of brief quotations embodied in critical reviews and certain other noncommercial uses permitted by copyright law.

Cover photo by Katelyn Elizabeth Oliver

Cover model: Meghan Chadeayne

Prologue

April woke up in someone's bed, alone. She looked around and assessed the room. It had flowery wallpaper and a large vanity in the corner. Sitting up, she was still in her bra and shorts and still bloody, though the blood had dried into a brown crust on her skin. She climbed out of the bed and opened the door. In the hallway, she heard a TV coming from another room. She walked into the living room to see an old woman sitting on a couch, with several of the children sitting around playing.

The kids had all been cleaned up and were wearing different clothes. The woman looked up at her.

"Oh! You're awake!" she said.

"Where am I?"

"I'm Mrs. Reynolds. You're in my home. Coy brought

you here."

"Where is Coy?"

"He's out tending to some things. You slept a long time," Mrs. Reynolds said.

"How long?"

"About two days. I'm cooking dinner right now. Got a nice roast in the oven. Why don't you get cleaned up and dinner will be ready. You could use it I'm sure. Coy said you'd really been through the ringer."

"Yeah, I have." Though the whole incident at the Funhouse felt like a crazy dream, but it had been all too real. "Where is Coy?" Coy had been the one to drag her and her friends to the Funhouse, but he went back to help her escape. He was too late for any of her friends though.

"He had to go take care of some things. There's clothes in the closet there that should fit you. Some of my daughter's clothes. Get you out of those rags."

"Yeah. Thank you," April said as she headed back to

the bedroom. She undressed and climbed into the shower. Blood ran down the drain as it washed off her. She washed her hair and body until all the blood and dirt was gone. Once she was clean, she stepped out and wrapped a towel around herself. After the shower, she felt like a new person. Looking at herself in the mirror, she brushed her black hair and found some women's jeans and a t-shirt in the closet.

Once she was dressed she headed back to the living room but followed the smell into the dining room. There was Mrs. Reynolds seated at the table with the children seated around, some were in booster seats.

"There you are! You look so pretty!" Mrs. Reynolds said.

"Thank you," April said. Looking at her plate, there was some cut up roast, steamed broccoli, mashed potatoes and a can of Diet Coke.

"You're probably pretty hungry."

"Starving," April said.

"Well don't wait around. You need your strength. Go ahead and eat, dear."

April sat down and dug into the roast. Each bite was juicy and tender. It was cooked to perfection. She scarfed down the meat, the potatoes, and broccoli and washed it all down with the Diet Coke. She sat the can down and looked up at Mrs. Reynolds.

"Wow, you were hungry," the old woman said.

"Yeah, I guess I was."

"How was it, dear?"

"Oh it was great. Thank you."

"Oh good. I'm so glad. My daughter always loved my roast."

"Yeah. Where is your daughter anyway? Does she still live around here?"

"No. I'm afraid not," Mrs. Reynolds said, setting her fork down.

"She move away?" April asked.

"No. You killed her you little cunt."

No sooner did Mrs. Reynolds speak when April began to feel lightheaded. At first just a little, but suddenly the room began to spin. She tried to stand, but stumbled to the floor, trying to hold herself up against the table.

"How'd you like them roofies, bitch?" Mrs. Reynolds said as she came around the table, standing over April. "My daughter went out there to help save you and your friends. I told her not to go, but she wanted to help. Always was a tomboy. Well you cut her in half with that goddamn chainsaw. Couldn't just kill the clowns. You had to kill everyone. My daughter, my friends. Now there's just a few of us left in this town." She paused to give April a feeble kick in the side. "Everyone in this town isn't bad! We're not murderers! You saw those clowns and what they could do. You think we liked them lording over us for all these years? You think we enjoyed grabbing travelers and their kids and forcing them into that place? The few times one of us didn't do it, we disappeared. No thank you."

"You really thought I was gonna take care of you?

You're not nearly as smart as Coy thought. Though he always was kinda slow. How you feelin? Got the spins yet?"

The woman kept talking, but April couldn't tell what she was saying. It all turned to gibberish as things kept spinning faster and faster until everything went dark. Right before she passed out, she wished she had killed Coy.

Chapter 1

April awoke, her vision foggy as her head pounded a thumping pain as if a little man with a sledge hammer were standing inside her skull bashing away. As her wits came about her, she tried to rub her head but couldn't move her hands. They were suspended above her, tied around a beam with plastic zip ties. Looking around, she realized she was in a barn and completely naked.

"Oh fuck. Not again," she muttered as she took in the situation. Her life had descended into an ongoing nightmare. She'd seen and done things in the past couple years that most would need decades of therapy in order to recover. She struggled against her bindings as much as she could, but they cut into her wrists which were already bleeding.

It was then and there she decided she would kill Coy. Not just kill him, but brutalize him in the most horrific ways she could think of. How stupid of her to trust that redneck asshole. He was the whole reason they'd ended up in the Funhouse to begin with. Fucking redneck goatfucker.

"Oh look! You're finally awake, huh bitch?" A girl said from the doorway. She came inside glaring at April. The girl was rail thin, with long, blonde hair and wearing a t-shirt and shorts that were both way too small.

"Who the fuck are you?" April asked.

The girl walked up to her, looked her up and down before slapping her across the face. The slap stung as her eyes watered while her cheek throbbed.

"You're gonna learn some respect you fucking cunt! You killed my whole family. You think you can just come in here with your big tits and tight ass and destroy our way of life?"

"Your 'family' forced us into that fucking Funhouse from hell. So yeah, I killed whoever I had to in order to survive. All my friends were murdered in there!" April said.

"Fuck you and your friends." The girl said and

punched her in the stomach. The blow took the wind from April as she tried to double over, gasping for air. "Fucking hurts don't it! My name is Candi Jean. I want you to remember that so you'll know who fucking killed you."

"Where's Coy and Mrs. Reynolds?" April asked.

"Mrs. Reynolds is busy. Coy, you won't see him again. He told me about your little mind trick. I was willing to bet it don't work on girls. Am I right?"

April looked down, refusing to reply.

"Ha! I knew it! Good. So don't expect to see him or any other guys you can fuck with anytime soon. Yeah you're pretty and have a bangin' body, but you won't be once I'm finished with you."

"I'm going to kill you with my bare hands." April said. "And make sure you feel every second of it."

"Yeah, good luck with that bitch." Candi Jean said as she turned and walked toward the door. "I'll be back soon. So don't go nowhere." She laughed as she disappeared through the door and slammed it shut.

Fucking cunt. April couldn't help but wonder how and why she always ended up with these crazy ass rednecks. She swore if she made it out of there, she was never leaving Austin again, and probably not even her house. Being a hermit was much safer than this chaos. Her face still stung from the slap. For a little skinny chick that girl was strong.

For the next hour at least April tried to distract herself from whatever was about to happen to her. She had escaped much worse situations, so no reason she couldn't get out this time. Unless of course they just up and killed her which she doubted. Finally Candi Jean came walking back in, looking as smug as she had earlier.

"You ready to play bitch?" Candi Jean said.

"Sure. Untie me and we can play real good."

"Nice try, but I don't think so. You're fine where you are. So tell me. How does this little trick of yours work? The jacking guys off with your brain? You learn that or something?"

"I don't know what you're talking about." April said.

Candi Jean slapped her across the other side of her face.

"Don't play dumb with me you stupid bitch! You know exactly what the fuck I'm talking about. How do you do that thing you do with men?"

"I don't know. I just up and did it one day, on accident. Then I realized I could control it. I have no idea how I actually did it."

"Yeah whatever. Don't matter. Coy said it only works on guys. So you won't be controlling me you fucking bitch. Maybe it works out of your pussy."

"I can assure you," April said. "My pussy has nothing to do with it."

"Well I guess we should find out," Candi Jean said as she dug into her bag and pulled a stun gun. April tried not to visibly cringe as she knew exactly what the girl had in mind with it. Walking up to her, Candi Jean took the stun gun and jammed it between April's legs, the jolt instantly sending pain through her as if her body were on fire. The spark fired right against her vagina, feeling as though her girl parts were being ripped out by a set of pliers. That probably would have been preferable.

After a few seconds, Candi Jean let up.

"How's that feel cunt? That tickle? Getting you all nice and wet?"

"You're so fucking dead," April said.

"Yeah. Not looking that way, huh bitch? How's that snatch feeling? Kinda twitchy? Tingly? How about another?"

Candi Jean jammed it back against her pussy and activated the stun gun yet again. April did everything she could to keep from showing pain, but it was near impossible. She didn't cry out at least. Wasn't going to give that little bitch the satisfaction of hearing her scream. Despite her best efforts though, a few screams did come out. Candi Jean stopped and pulled it away as she backed up.

"See bitch? That's just the start. When I get back, we'll have some real fun!" She said as she grabbed her bag and headed out. Once the door slammed shut, April closed her eyes and took a deep breath. Tears she had been holding back started to flow. She didn't want to cry, but at least it wouldn't be in front of that crazy bitch. One thought that gave her comfort, was thinking of all the ways she planned to kill Candi Jean.

Chapter 2

Isis Raine sped down the highway trying to clear her head. She couldn't believe that asshole. After she gave him two years of her life, he just decides to bang some skank at the club? She knew she didn't like him bouncing at a strip club, but figured she could trust him. So much for that idea. The thought of the whole thing made her blood boil.

Most her life, she had been prone to blow ups, but in recent years they had gotten worse. She'd been told she had narcisstic personality disorder by one of her professors the short time she was in college, so she knocked the bitch out. That got her expelled, but they didn't bother pressing charges. Since then, they only got worse. Her boyfriend had put up with it for a while, but he said he was getting sick of it. Well, tough shit. He knew what he was getting into. Though maybe killing him was a bit much, but he deserved it. The fucker had made her a promise! Ok, breathe.

She stomped on the brakes as the tires screeched to a halt just missing the car in front of her. Once she caught her breath, Isis looked around. The traffic had come to a standstill.

"Goddammit. Go!" She screamed as if that would make traffic move faster. She took out her frustration on the steering wheel, punching it repeatedly. Slowly cars creeped along a few feet at a time. Just ahead there was an exit ramp. She pulled onto the shoulder and sped toward the ramp, ignoring the rumble strips as she pulled off the highway. The access road would be much faster, it had to be. Plus the cops would be less likely looking for her on that route.

Though she got down the access road a short way before she hit a "Road Closed" sign.

"Motherfucker!" She shouted. This was starting to piss her off. She turned down the detour and sped along. Turning up the stereo, she began blasting The Panic Beats through the speakers. Maybe the punk songs about murder and mayhem fed into her rage, but she didn't really give a fuck. As she raced down the road, she didn't notice the "Welcome to Happytown" sign.

It did get her attention when she rolled through the little town and there were some older women and younger girls. They were standing along the road crying while someone with a dump truck crept down the street. She pulled right up behind the truck, just as many of the women began screaming at her. Some started throwing things at her car. She slammed on the brakes and jumped out of the car, getting in one of the younger lady's face.

"Are you out of your fucking mind throwing shit at my car?"

"You just drove right up in our funeral procession you stupid bitch!" The woman screamed.

"Funeral procession? That's a fucking dump truck—" Her voice trailed off as she looked and for the first time noticed the contents of the dump truck was a pile of dead bodies. Some were just body parts, all of them were mangled and mutilated. "What the fuck?"

"Yeah. Funeral. If I were you, I'd get back in your car and go back the way you came." The woman said as one of the older ones came walking over. All of the women were looking her up and down. She was used to such looks wearing her cut off Misfits t-shirt and cut off jean shorts and jet black hair pulled into a pony tail. Her left arm sported a half sleeve of tattoos as well as a large tattoo of a tiger on her right thigh.

"What's the problem over here?" The old lady said.

"This bitch comes driving all up in our funeral procession now she wants to run her mouth."

"What happened to all those people? Why are they in a dump truck?" Isis asked.

"Don't you worry yourself with how we handle our business young lady. You should just get on out of here."

Isis took a deep breath, trying to keep from going off.

"Look, I'm just trying to get to Dallas. The road is closed. I can't go back that way because the road is closed."

"Well, we need to honor our dead and lay them to rest. There's a diner just down the street. Why don't you park and I'll take you there for some coffee while we finish up. Then you can get on your way." The old woman explained.

Isis didn't want to hang out at some hick diner and drink coffee, she wanted to get far, far away from here. But she didn't want to get into a fight during their fucked up funeral or whatever this was. Something seriously was wrong with a dump truck full of dead bodies, and she didn't want to stick around to find out. But if it got them off her back, hopefully it wouldn't be long before she could go.

"All right I guess," Isis said. "Where is this place?"

"Follow me dear," the old woman said.

As they walked the woman tried to chat Isis up, but she wasn't really interested in being her pal. The woman did say her name was Agnes Jameson, not that Isis gave a shit. Once in the café, Agnes sat down with her and brought her a cup of coffee.

"So what brings you to Happytown? You seem angry." Agnes asked.

"Just had a lot of shit going on. So I needed to get away. What the hell kind of name is Happytown? Especially when you all have a dump truck filled with dead bodies."

Agnes sat her coffee down and took a deep breath.

"Something really awful happened here a few days ago. A lot of men lost their lives as a result. Most the men in this town died. So we are left to clean up and move on as best we can. It's been over a hundred degrees out last few days, so can't just leave them lying out in the heat. So we are doing a mass burial."

"What happened exactly?" Isis asked.

"It's a lot to explain and not worth your trouble dear. Go ahead and finish your coffee. She sipped at the warm drink, though coffee wasn't something she cared for. This one had a funny after taste to it. She took another sip before she sat it down and jumped up.

"You old bitch! You trying to drug me?" Isis yelled.

"No hun, settle down. Why would I do that?"

"Why do you have a dump truck full of dead bodies out there?"

"I told you…"

"Yeah, bullshit."

She turned and headed to the door when a group of women came storming in, some of them carrying two by fours and crowbars. She grabbed a fork from a table and turned to run toward the kitchen. Agnes tried to jump in her way, but she jammed the fork into her throat without hesitating. Agnes clutched her neck as she gagged and gurgled before falling to the ground. The women gave chase as Isis ran through the kitchen, where she grabbed a meat cleaver before running out the back door.

Isis ran between houses and turned right as mob of women pursued her. She ducked behind some bushes as she listened to them screaming and shouting.

"Come on out bitch! You can't hide from us!" One of them screamed. Isis had never backed out of a fight, but she knew she didn't stand a chance against a mob of crowbar wielding bitches. She crept around the house, looking into the window. It appeared empty, so she made her way to the side of the house where she checked the door. It was unlocked. Opening it slowly she stepped inside. Holding the cleaver at the ready she checked each of the rooms.

"Mommy! Is that you?" A voice called out. She turned as a little girl, around ten years old came running into the room, almost hugging Isis until she froze and looked up at her. "Hey! Where's my mom?"

Instead of a reply, Isis brought down the cleaver.

Chapter 3

Coy drove the dump truck out past the town limits and to the burial site he'd prepared earlier. This had to be one of the more crude burials he'd ever seen, but the best way he could think to take care of hundreds of bodies. Loading them into the truck had been traumatic though. Especially when he got to Old Man Gunn. His head had been ripped clean off. He found it a few dozen feet away from the body, but it had been smashed like a pumpkin.

He'd put the clown bodies into a pile and set them on fire. The Funhouse remained untouched. No one had gone inside, and he wasn't even sure if there were any clowns still in there or not. Though he'd doubted it. He thought he'd seen a couple clowns driving away during the fight, but wasn't sure. Either way, the Funhouse had been silent since that day.

Then there was that April girl. He'd really liked her, but Mrs. Reynolds wasn't too happy about her killing most of the town. Sure, the girl was upset at them for dragging them into that place to be tortured and killed. He'd probably be mad too. So Mrs. Reynolds locked her in her barn and turned Candi Jean loose on her. That girl was crazy as hell anyway. They wouldn't let him go near April after her weird brain sex control powers she could do.

He wanted to see her though, he liked her. Not just because she was pretty. There was just something about her, and when she jacked him off with her brain, that felt really good too. He just didn't like her controlling him after. Once he reached the large grave, he backed the truck up to the edge and pulled the lever as the bucket raised, dumping its contents into the hole.

Once the truck was empty, he pulled it away and hopped out. It sucked he had to do all the work, but most of the women in town were used to taking care of things at home while the men did most of the hard work. Some of the younger ladies didn't mind getting their hands dirty, but it was just the way of things in Happytown.

He climbed into the backhoe and began scooping large piles of dirt into the hole. Before long, there was a mound of fresh dirt, marking the mass grave. Once he had it filled in, he parked the backhoe and climbed back into the dump truck, heading back to town. As he pulled in, several women were running through the streets carrying pipes and clubs. He pulled up Jenny Adams and rolled the window down.

"What in the hell is goin' on?" Coy asked.

"Some outsider bitch came driving through here and disrupted the funeral." Jenny said. She was waving a metal pipe around as she spoke. He'd never seen her looking so angry.

"Yeah I saw a car behind me for a bit. Why so mad though? It's not like we gotta take her to the Funhouse."

"It don't matter. I'm gonna beat that bitch's skull in!" Jenny said as she ran off. Coy watched as the women ran up and down through the streets. Whoever this girl was, they must've been looking for her. He drove the truck down town and parked it. Another woman, Grace Ellis ran up to him.

"You seen her?" Grace asked.

"The outsider girl?"

"Yeah."

"I don't even know what she looks like."

"Like some city rocker chick. Jean shorts, black shirt, ponytail. Has tattoos on her legs, the dirty skank." Grace said.

"Nah. I just got back from burying the bodies. I missed all this commotion."

"I found her!" Someone screamed a few houses down. "I found her! She's…" The scream was cut off. Everyone ran in that direction as Coy followed along. He was mostly curious as to what the commotion was all about. They arrived at one of the houses where the front door was open.

"They're fucking dead!" Someone screamed. Coy pushed his way past and into the house. The first thing he saw was the little girl, he couldn't remember her name, but the child lie on the ground with her face split open. Chunks of brains and skull oozed out of a hole where her face used to be. Not far away was another woman. She was lying on her side, with her head at an awkward angle. Though her head was that way because it was almost chopped off. It clung to her neck by a few pieces of skin and muscle.

"Jesus Christ!" Coy said. "What happened?"

"That outsider bitch killed them both." Jenny said from behind him.

"I see that. Where is she?"

"She ran off again."

"Well shit. We better find her." He said as he turned.

"I'm gonna get Zeus so we can find this bitch." Zeus was his German shepherd. Coy had gotten him as a puppy and had taught him to track. As far as he was concerned, Zeus was as good as any police dog. After what he just saw, he wanted to get his hands on that bitch himself. He couldn't get the image of that poor little girl with her face split open out of his head. Who would do something like that?

The more he thought about it, the angrier he got. Over the past few days, he'd seen more blood, guts and dead bodies than he'd ever cared to. But this, children? It was too much. Once he got home, he sat down and put his head in his hands. Over the past few days, he hadn't stopped to think about all that had happened. Suddenly it was hitting him all at once. He took some deep breaths as he went out back where Zeus was running around. The dog ran up to him as he knelt down and scratched the dog's ears.

"Hey boy! How's my big boy huh?"

Zeus panted as his master scratched his ears and neck.

"You wanna go hunt down a bitch for me? Do ya? Yeah, let's go boy. Let's go get her."

Chapter 4

April had to think. That Candi Jean bitch would be back anytime and God knows what kind of horrors she was about to unleash. The ties on her wrists were cutting into her flesh, as blood seeped out of the wounds. She could barely feel her fingers at this point. No way was she slipping her hands out of that mess.

There had been a bunch of screaming and yelling from outside earlier. It was a bunch of women. She had no idea what they were screaming over, but it had quieted down for a moment. April wished more than anything that her ability worked on women as well as men. Maybe there was a way, but she had no idea how. She barely understood how it worked on men.

There was some more banging around outside when the door swung open again. Candi Jean had returned. This time she was carrying a duffel bag. Fuck.

"Ready to play bitch?" Candi Jean said. "We're gonna have us some fun! At least, I'll have fun. You, not so much." She dug through the bag and took out a large dildo. Actually, calling large was an understatement. The thing was huge. "You're about to get fucked." Candi Jean said.

April wasn't about to let her come near her with that thing. As Candi Jean came closer, April waited until she was right in front of her before lifting both legs and kicking Candi Jean in the stomach, knocking her across the room. Candi Jean dropped the dildo as she fell. What little sense of satisfaction April may have had was short lived, however. Candi Jean quickly jumped to her feet.

"That was really fuckin' stupid," she said as she walked up to April again, this time from the side and punched her in the face. April's teeth clacked together as her vision went blank for a second. It came back, but she was woozy and seeing stars. Before she could say anything, Candi Jean punched her again. This time she almost lost consciousness. That was the last thing she wanted to do. No telling what Candi Jean would do to her if she passed out.

After a minute or two, her vision started to clear as

she tasted her own blood inside her mouth as well as blood oozing from her nose.

"You done being stupid?" Candi Jean asked. April just glared at her. "I asked you a question bitch!"

April stared, for a moment and then spit a wad of blood and saliva into Candi Jean's face. The girl took a step back, first in shock, then rage. April knew it was stupid and she was about to really get it. But there was no way she was going to let this cunt break her.

Candi Jean wiped her face off before digging out a large plastic bag. April immediately knew what she was going to do, and began to struggle. There was no way she was moving though. Candi Jean took the bag and circled around behind her.

"You think you're funny bitch?" Candi Jean said.

"Fuck you."

"Yeah. You'll wish you just let me play instead of acting like a stupid cunt."

"I'm going to get out of here. And I will cut your tits

off and feed them to you." April said.

Candi Jean just laughed at the threat.

"Now that is funny. That's funny as shit. You ain't goin' nowhere." Candi Jean said as she put the bag over April's head. April took in a deep breath as the bag went over her head, but in a few seconds she was running out of air. She finally tried to take a breath only to get nothing. Struggling against Candi Jean, she whipped her head from side to side, trying to create an opening for air.

Her body violently reacted by jerking and kicking all over. The only thing that mattered was a breath of air. She had heard drowning was the worst way to die. Suffocating was pretty fucking bad on its own. She began feeling lightheaded as she continued gasping desperately for air. Finally Candi Jean lifted the bag from her head as air filled April's lungs. She took several deep breaths as her eyes came back into focus.

"You like that shit bitch?" Candi Jean asked. "You learning some manners?"

April began to speak but it came out as a whisper.

"What'd you say?" Candi Jean asked.

April repeated it, but her voice was barely audible. Candi Jean leaned in closer.

"Speak up bitch! You talk like you got a dick in your mouth."

April turned her head around and bit into Candi Jean's nose. The girl screamed as April sank her teeth in as blood filled her mouth. Candi Jean struggled against her, swinging and punching wildly but April didn't loosen her grip in the slightest. Finally Candi Jean was able to wiggle her way out, but only after leaving a chunk of her nose in April's mouth.

Candi Jean stumbled away with both hands over her face.

"You bitch!" She screamed. "You fucking bitch! You bit off my nose!"

April spit the chunk of meat from her mouth and looked over at Candi Jean.

"Yeah I did. And you taste like shit you inbred fuck,"

April said.

"My nose! You fucking bit off my nose! I'll kill you! I'll fucking kill you!" She screamed as she ran out of the barn. There was a trail of blood marking Candi Jean's path once she was gone. April felt somewhat amused at herself she was able to fuck that girl up so badly she ran off crying. No doubt she'd be back and likely kill her, but April no longer cared. After everything she'd been through in the past week, death would be a welcome relief.

The door to the barn creaked open again as April braced herself for another round of Candi Jean. Except it wasn't her. It was a different girl. This one obviously wasn't from around here.

"What in the fuck?" The girl said.

"My thoughts exactly," April answered.

"Why are you all tied up and naked?""

"I can tell you're not one of these assholes by the way you're dressed. So since you're not here to kill me, could you cut me loose please? Before psycho comes back?" April said.

"Is this what they do when they catch you?"

"Among other things. Cut me loose please?"

"Oh, right," the girl said as she looked around until she found a knife in the bag. Walking over to April she cut the ties off her wrists. April lowered her hands, rubbing them together as feeling slowly began to return.

"Thank you. We gotta get out of here," April said.

"Shit. I came in here to hide."

"Yeah, bad idea. This whole town is fucked up. We need to get out of here. Do you have a car?"

"Yeah. Its downtown if we can get to it," the girl said.

"Shit. We'll figure something out." April looked around for something to wear so she wouldn't be streaking through town. Unfortunately there was nothing in the barn for her to put on. "Fuck it. Let's get out of here. I'm April by the way."

"Isis. Nice to meet you, I think."

Chapter 5

Grant Storm sped along the back roads, getting closer to his destination. This one should be easy. He was certain she had no idea what she was, or that he was coming. Those were the easiest to get close to. This girl's name was April Kennedy. He glanced down at the folder on his passenger seat and pulled out her picture. She was a looker, there was no doubt about that. He'd been tracking neuropaths for thirty years. This one was the most attractive by far and the most dangerous.

Most neuros had the ability to control minds, that's what made them neuros. This one has a sexual component to her, one like he'd never seen before. In the past two years she'd taken out two small towns on her own. It was his job to make sure it was her last.

How he located her was a sordid and complicated tale. Most neuros come into their abilities by accident and have no idea how to control it. From there it's just a matter of time until word gets back to the Trackers whose job it is to find and eliminate them. A lot had changed over the years. In the early days, Trackers would capture them to be studied. Most of the time with horrific results.

The worst was back in the eighties in the old Soviet Union, one of them had gotten away and was captured by the KGB. As one would expect from the Soviets, they tried to turn him into a weapon. The neuro killed dozens of soldiers before they finally put him down. After that, it was decided they were too dangerous. Death was the only solution

The Trackers were above and beyond any government. Most governments didn't even know they existed. They operated in the shadows, yet in plain sight all around the world. Grant mostly covered the southwest United States and California. Occasionally he'd bring in other Trackers if things got too crazy. Most of the time he did just fine on his own. The key was getting close to them before they knew you were there. If they saw you coming or if you make your move and failed, they had you. He'd seen many Trackers fall to neuros over the years. It was never pretty. One neuro made a tracker cut his own face off and eat it. No thank you.

No one knows exactly where neuros come from. Their abilities are genetic and usually take hold in early adulthood. It almost always occurs during or after some severe trauma or crisis. So it's possible there are neuros out there who live their whole lives and never know it and never gain their abilities. In April's case, her captivity would have been more than enough to launch her ability.

His last bit of information he'd gotten on April was she was located in some backwoods town called Happytown. For some reason he imagined the place was a miserable little hell hole. Most small towns were, at least underneath. They put on a nice façade of being the next Mayberry. But beneath the surface, there was always something much darker. Happytown would be no different.

After a few more miles he drove past the Happytown city limit sign. As he cruised through the little downtown area, it didn't look much different than all the other small towns he'd visited. This place was much quieter though. At one corner there was a large group of women gathered around. Many were holding bats, axes and one had a rake. April was here all right. She had to be. He pulled up to the women and turned off the truck.

Every one of them stopped and glared at him as he climbed out. He put on his Stetson and stepped out of the pickup.

"Afternoon ladies," he said as they looked him up and down. He adjusted his aviators as he walked toward them. "I'm Grant Storm. Texas Rangers." He took out his badge and I.D. and held it up to the women. It was all fake, but would check out if someone were to look into it. He had credentials for almost all major law enforcement agencies.

"What do you want?" One of the older women said. "No one here called the law!"

"No ma'am. But the law is here regardless. I'm looking for this woman." He held up April's photo. Immediately he saw the recognition in their eyes. They tried to mask it, but it was there. He was sure of it.

"No sir. None of us seen that girl. We don't welcome

outsiders here. Not even the law," the woman said.

"I can tell you this. I'm not leaving until I find her, and I know for fact she's here. So if you don't care to help me, I'll look around myself."

"I don't think you wanna do that Ranger. The law leaves us alone and we tend to our own affairs. That's how it's always been."

Grant looked around for a moment and considered the situation.

"Where's all your men at?" He asked.

"Huh?"

"Your men. Where are they?"

"They're at work, like workin' men should be!" The woman cackled.

"I don't think so. She killed them, didn't she?"

The women looked at each other uncomfortably before the old woman spoke up again.

"Not to mention, by the look of your tools there I'm guessing you weren't headed to a gardening party. Unless there's something you can plant with ball bats," he said.

"Now look! I'm not gonna warn you again--" She screamed. Before she could finish, he drew his Desert Eagle .44 magnum and shot the woman in the face. Her head exploded like a melon as blood and brains sprayed the crowd of women who were already screaming. A few started toward him, but he already had the gun pointed at the group.

"That's as far as any of you go! I tried to be nice about this, but you ladies wanted to make it difficult. Now once again, that girl's name is April Kennedy. Any of you seen her?" He said.

Before anyone could answer, another girl came running up. She was short with blonde hair, and had a bloody hole where her nose should have been.

"She's gone! That fucking bitch that bit my nose off is gone!" The girl screamed.

"I bet that other one cut her loose," another woman

said.

The girl noticed the old woman's body for the first time and froze, as she looked up at Grant.

"Who the fuck are you?" She said.

"That man is a Texas Ranger," the woman said. "He's gonna help us kill these bitches."

Chapter 6

Coy followed behind Zeus as the dog ran from house to house seeking out the outsider. Part of him hoped if he helped find the girl, the women of the town would take him more seriously as the man of the town. Maybe he could take several of them as wives. He could think of a few ladies he wouldn't mind taking as his wives. Up until the past few days, he was just big, dumb Coy. Now he was literally the only guy in town.

Zeus took off running and turned a corner. Coy tried to keep up with him, but the dog was too fast. He must be on to something.

"Zeus! Come back here! Zeus!" He called out.

Coy ran around the building and stopped as there was Zeus lying on his back while April who happened to be naked knelt by him rubbing his belly. There was another girl standing next to April.

"Oh shit," Coy said.

April looked up at him, and instantly his dick became rock hard.

"No! No! Don't do this! Please!" He begged.

"You handed me over to that old hag to have me tortured you fuck! Your ass is mine!"

He wanted to turn and run away, but he couldn't. Plus his dick felt so good as his balls began to tingle as he grew harder and harder in his jeans. So hard, that he undid his jeans and took his dick out, watching it throb. The girl with April looked on with bizarre fascination.

"What is going on?" The girl asked.

"Just watch," April said.

In a matter of seconds a wave of intense pleasure swept over Coy as he ejaculated. Even though April was almost ten feet away, his load almost hit her. She had to duck out of the way as it shot over her head.

"Holy shit!" The other girl said as Coy collapsed to the ground.

Coy gasped for air as the ground felt as if it were spinning beneath him. April walked over and stood over him. She looked even more beautiful than the last time he'd seen her. The fact that she was naked didn't hurt. Her body was a work of art.

"Get up," she said. Without realizing what he was doing he stood. She'd done this to him once before, inside the Funhouse. She was now in control of her mind.

"Look, I'm sorry. I didn't know what Mrs. Reynolds was gonna do to you!" Coy said.

"Right. That's the second time you led me to my death but you were totally innocent and helpless. Right?"

"Well yes, I mean no….I mean…."

"Shut up. Play with your dick for me."

Immediately he back jacking off again. In seconds he was hard.

"Good Now go fuck your dog in the ass," she ordered.

"Please don't make me do this," he said as he walked over to Zeus who was now sitting upright. He pushed up the dog's rear end and slid his cock into the dog's asshole. The dog yelped and whined as Coy slid his cock in and out.

"Oh my God!" The other girl squealed. "How are you doing this?"

"Just a little thing I learned," April said.

"Holy shit! You're really making him fuck a dog. It's so gross, but I can't stop looking."

Coy continued to hump away as the dog whined and even began howling. Finally Coy finished, shooting his load inside the dog's ass. He pulled out, fell to the ground and threw up. Zeus began lapping up his vomit as he stood. He had to look away before he puked again. Tears ran down his face as he fastened his jeans.

"Now, you're coming with us. Bring Zeus. It's too bad I had to put him through that," April said.

"Put him through it?"

"Yeah. No creature should have to have your pathetic dick inside of them. Now, give me your shirt."

Without a word, he unbuttoned his work shirt and handed it to her. She put it on and buttoned it up and began walking. Coy followed her as Zeus and the other girl trailed along.

"So who is your friend?" Coy asked.

"You mean the girl you were sending your dog after? That's Isis."

"Cool name."

"Shut the fuck up."

"Damn. You got a way with men don't you?" Isis said.

"You could say that," April said.

"You'll have to teach me that trick."

"So what are you gonna do with me?" Coy asked.

"First thing is you'll help us get out of here. After that, I'll have you kill yourself in the most horrible way I can think of."

Coy's stomach tightened at her words. How could she be so casual talking about killing him? Or forcing him to kill himself? Though he saw how effortlessly she killed at the Funhouse. He should have taken her to safety instead of selling her out to Mrs. Reynolds. He figured he would be improving his standing in the town. Instead he was ending his own life.

"That really shut him up," Isis said.

"So where is a car?" April asked.

"Go to the end of these houses and to your right. My truck will be right around there," Coy said.

They did as he said and there it was. His pickup truck sitting outside a house. They ran across the street and reached the truck.

"Keys," April said.

Coy dug in his pocket and handed her his keys. As April was opening the door, from behind her someone racked a shotgun.

"Stop right there," a woman said. April slowly turned to see a middle aged woman pointing a shotgun at them. Isis looked around as Coy just stood there.

"Why are you helping them?" The woman asked Coy.

"Well, I'm not--" he began.

"Coy." April interrupted as Coy began to move once again against his own will. Before the woman holding the gun could react, he stepped up to her, grabbed the shotgun from her hands and struck her in the face with the butt. She screamed as she fell to the ground.

"I'm real sorry," Coy said. "She's making me do it. I can't help myself." He continued smashing her in the face with the butt of the shotgun. Over and over the stock slammed into her face until her head split open, spilling its contents of brains, bone and fluid onto the sidewalk.

"Holy shit!" Isis said. "Did you see her fuckin' head bust open? Shit that was awesome."

April glared at her as Isis shut up. Coy stood there holding the shotgun and looking at the woman's body.

He held up the gun, pointing the barrel under his chin. April looked over just in time, forcing him to lower it.

"Not so fast, cowboy. I'm not done with you yet."

Chapter 7

April ordered Coy into the bed of the truck as she and Isis climbed into the cab. She started it as the engine roared to life. Thank God. It was time to get out of this armpit of a town. Throwing the truck into drive, she stepped on the gas while pulling onto the street. She did a U-turn, driving up onto the curb as she turned the truck around to head out of the town.

The streets were quiet as they cruised through town. That is, until just before the city limits where a mob of women was gathered. She stomped on the gas, picking up speed as one of the women jumped into the middle of the street, shaking her fist and shouting something. April didn't slow down as the pickup struck the woman who exploded upon impact. At least that's what it looked like.

Her head and limbs went flying as the rest of her body rolled under the truck. Entrails splattered against the windshield as Isis screamed.

"Jesus fuck! You are crazy!" She said.

"Don't I know it," April responded. She turned on the wipers to wipe away the guts on the windshield, but it only formed thick red streaks. From the side of the road, someone threw a brick at the truck, shattering the driver's side window. The brick struck April in the head as she lost control of the truck. It swerved and bucked as the truck veered off the road and smashed into a street light.

April jerked to a stop against her seatbelt, knocking the wind out of her. The airbag blasted her in the face causing her to see stars. As her head cleared Isis was looking at dazed as she felt. Coy was lying on the ground face down a few feet in front of the pickup and Zeus was next to him, sniffing at his body. April couldn't tell if he was alive or dead. She stumbled out of the truck as the women stood glaring at her as if they were about to rip the flesh off her bones.

Another pickup came pulling up and screeched to a halt about a hundred feet away. She wasn't sure who it was or why they were stopping there, but she wasn't about to stick around and find out. She took off running in between some houses. Isis ran behind her as they wove through houses.

"What's going on?" Isis called out.

"I don't know. We got to find another way out of here." April was so livid. They were so close to getting out of there. It's as if she'd died and gone to hell, and this place was it. She'll spend eternity trying to escape these assholes only to be dragged back into the town somehow. If she believed in hell, she might believe that's where she was. But she didn't, and it wasn't. Getting out of trouble had become her specialty as of late, and she wasn't going to give up now.

There was no one immediately behind them as they wove through some houses and into a wooded area. April's bare feet stung at the sticks and rocks she ran on, but she did her best to ignore the pain. Isis stumbled along behind her until they saw a cabin up ahead. April slowed and took cover behind some trees as they approached. There was no one outside the cabin. Looking back, she wasn't sure how far from town they'd come. They'd been running at least fifteen minutes.

There were voices coming from the town and getting louder.

"Sounds like the lynch mob is on the way," April said.

"What a bunch of crazy bitches. Where are all the men?"

"I killed them all."

"Holy shit. Are you serious? Who are you for real?"

"I told you, I'm April," she said as she crept slowly toward the cabin. She ducked down as she looked in the window. There was no one inside so she kept her head down as she snuck around back. In back was a woman leaned over a well pulling up a bucket. Before April could do anything, Isis appeared from the other side of the house, ran up behind the woman and shoved her down the well. The woman screamed as she fell and then was silent. April ran up to the well looking down. The woman was lying there partly submerged in water. April couldn't tell if she were alive or dead. Until the woman began screaming again.

"Help! Get me out of here!"

"What did you do that for?" April asked.

"I figured we needed the cabin. Shit you just used some mind control to make some guy split a girl's head open and fuck a dog. This is tame by comparison."

"Fair enough. She can't keep screaming like this."

Isis looked around and walked toward some large chunks of concrete blocks. She grabbed several and began hurling them at the woman in the well. She screamed as each lump of concrete bounced off her body with a sickening thud. April watched with morbid fascination as Isis grabbed brick after brick, winding up as if she were Nolan Ryan and firing it into the well.

Even after the woman stopped screaming and moving, Isis continued throwing them. April finally grabbed her and pulled her off.

"Jesus!" April said. "I think she's fucking dead."

Isis took some deep breaths before putting her arms down and walking away.

"What the hell was that? Why'd you push her down there?"

"She's one of them! Can't you tell?" Isis said.

"We don't know that."

"After what they did to you? You trust any of them?"

"Good point," April said. "Let's go see what she's got in here."

The back door was part way open as they walked inside. April walked into one of the back rooms and there was a small closet. She grabbed a pair of shorts and a t-shirt and put them on. The shorts were ok, the shirt was a little small, but would work. There was also a pair of sock and shoes that were slightly too big, but big enough. At least she wouldn't be barefoot.

"Holy shit!" Isis called out. "Check this shit out."

April ran into the other room next to a large cabinet where Isis was staring at like a kid at the ice cream truck.

"Jesus Christ!" April said as she looked up and down

an entire arsenal of weapons. There were long guns, hand guns, boxes and boxes of ammo and knives of various sizes. Hanging on the inner door of the cabinet was a large sword in a sheath. April pulled the sword down and slid it out of the sheath. It was a broadsword. Heavy, but not clumsy the weight felt good in her hands. She took a few practice swings with it before she noticed Isis glaring at her.

"Seriously?" Isis said. "A fuckin' sword?"

"I used to play with practice swords with my dad. Besides, I cut people up with a machete. A sword should be even better."

"Jesus you're a crazy bitch."

"So says the one who just threw some woman down a well and stoned her to death."

"Hey, that bitch would have killed us. Look at all this shit." Isis grabbed a shotgun and two small semi-automatic handguns. Looking around, Isis spotted a backpack in the corner of the room. She grabbed it and filled it with ammo boxes. There were a couple holsters for the handguns, Isis inserted the guns and clipped them to her waistband.

April slid the sword back into its sheath and slung it over around her back. There was a larger handgun hanging on the back of the cabinet. This was a .357 Colt Python. It wasn't new by any stretch. The holster looked dirty and worn, as the gun itself was covered in dirt and dust. She removed it and spun the barrel. It spun easily. There was fresh carbon on the inside as if it had been fired recently.

"You're gonna take that old thing?" Isis asked.

"Hey, my dad used to have one of these. They're good, reliable guns."

"Jesus Christ. I'm stuck in redneck town with Joan Wayne."

April laughed at Isis' play on words.

"I'll take that any day. We should keep moving before the mob gets here."

Chapter 8

Grant watched with amusement as the mob of women pursued the two girls. In the meantime, they'd left their one man left in town lying face down on the pavement. Grant walked over to the young man and knelt down. The guy was still moving.

"Hey hoss, you alive?" Grant asked as he shook the man. The guy stirred a little and began to sit up.

"Hmph," the man said as he rolled onto his back. His face was bloody and scraped up. "What happened?"

"Them girls threw you out of their truck when they crashed."

"What girls? Shit, my head hurts."

"Can you stand? I might need your help," Grant said. He didn't really need anyone's help, but figured he could use this guy as bait if he had to.

"I think so," the guy said as he slowly got to his feet.

He was a bit wobbly at first, but finally got his footing. "I remember now. God. Them bitches are evil."

"I know. I'm Grant. Grant Storm, Texas Rangers."

"I'm Coy. I'm the only man left in town. Well besides you that is."

"I figured. I been after the one girl for a while. April. She's extremely dangerous."

"Yeah. I gathered that," Coy said.

"Let's go. My truck is this way. They ran back that way through those houses. Anything back there?"

"Just more houses. Then the woods starts there. Those go on for a while," Coy explained.

Grant considered this for a moment.

"Is there a way to drive there?"

"Sure. I can show you."

"Great, hop in." Grant said as they climbed into Grant's truck and drove around the outside of town. Coy showed him a dirt road that ran around some of the larger properties to the edge of the woods. There was a dirt road that ran into the woods. Turning the truck onto the side road they were instantly surrounded by thick trees. After driving several more minutes, they heard gunfire coming from their right.

"Shit, sounds like they found 'em," Coy said.

"Could be."

"You got any extra guns?"

"Nope," Grant said as he pulled off the road, weaving through the trees until he could see some of the women surrounding a cabin. They were all exchanging gunfire. There were bodies of some of them lying around.

"Damn. This is crazy shit," Coy said.

"Sure is." Grant's cell phone began to ring as he slowed the pickup and pulled to a stop. He pressed it to his ear.

"Storm. What is your status?" The man on the other end asked. It was his boss, Chandler.

"Looks like the subject is cornered in a cabin. I'm getting ready to move in."

"Good. We got new orders on this one. They want her brought in."

"Brought in? Why? You see what she can do? How dangerous she is?"

"We're well aware. This one is unlike any other neuro we've seen. They want to study here. Is this some new evolution or a fluke?"

"Jesus. This is a really bad idea," Grant said.

"If you can't handle it, I can send someone who can."

"No. I got it. I just think it's a real bad idea."

"That's why we don't pay you to think. Make it happen," Chandler said and hung up.

"Shit," Grant said.

"What's wrong?"

"Nothing. Just slight change of plans."

Grant jumped out of the pickup and walked to the back. He lowered the tailgate and climbed into the bed. He opened the cargo chest and took out a small bag and a sonic devastator. It was something he'd built himself and modified over the years.

It looked like a science fiction ray gun, but with a large opening at the end. He put on ear plugs and over the ear protection as he set it up.

"What is that thing?" Coy asked.

"Just plug your ears," Grant said as he walked toward the cabin. He stopped about twenty feet behind the women shooting at the cabin, held up the sonic devastator and cranked the knob on the side. He could hardly hear it, but felt the vibration as he slowly turned the knob away from him. The women around the cabin all grabbed their ears and fell to the ground. Some were looking at him, one was even trying to point her gun at him, but he cranked the knob as far as it would go and she dropped it.

Holding the devastator out in front of him, he walked

toward the cabin and pushed the door open. There just inside the door were both women lying on the ground. He kept the sound cranked up as he approached April and sat down his bag and opened it up. He removed a small vial and a syringe, extracting a large dose of the drug. It was a barbiturate used to euthanize animals. In humans the right dose would put someone out for hours.

April was still conscious, but covering her ears and her mouth was open as if she were screaming. She probably was screaming, but he just couldn't hear her. As he approached, she tried kicking at him. Something he'd learned over the years, neuros couldn't function around high pitched sounds. He wasn't sure why, he was sure there was some scientific explanation. Whatever it was, all they could do was writhe and scream. That he could deal with.

He sat on April's legs as she tried to kick and put a knee on her stomach. Forcing her onto her side, he slid her shorts up slightly, injected the needle into her butt and pushed in the plunger. In a few seconds she was out. Grant put away the drugs and heaved April up over his shoulder. The other girl was lying not far away curled up into a fetal position. He stepped over her as he walked out carrying April.

He reached his truck and turned the sonic devastator off. He handcuffed April's hands behind her back and placed a black hood over her head, cinching it shut around the neck but not too tight. Once she was secure, he wrapped a sheet around her before covering her in a canvas tarp and fastened it to the truck bed.

"Wow, she's not going nowhere," Coy said.

"Nope. She probably won't wake up for a while, but in case she does, she's safe and secure."

"Whatcha gonna do with her. She made me fuck a dog!"

Grant looked at him and let out a short laugh.

"You musta pissed her off good. I can believe it though. Neuros are ruthless."

"Neuro?"

"Neuropath. It's what people like her are. Dangerous as hell. It's my job to find them and clean 'em up. She's a weird one though, so taking her in."

"In where?"

"Long story. Thanks for your help Coy. You won't have to worry about this one again. That I can promise," Grant said as he climbed into the pickup and started the engine. This job had gone easier than he'd suspected though. That worried him.

Chapter 9

Isis woke up to find herself strapped to a table. It was a kitchen table in a kitchen that smelled like fungus and rotten fish. She'd been stripped of her own clothes as she struggled against her restraints. Whoever tied her down, had done a good job of using belts and bungee cords. Her hands were almost numb, and she couldn't move at all against the straps around her forehead and neck.

As she struggled, a young blonde haired woman came walking in. This one had a huge piece of gauze over her nose.

"Well, someone is finally awake," the girl said.

"Where am I?"" Isis asked.

"Same place you always been bitch. You're in Happytown, though it's about to get real unhappy for you."

"Why are you people out to hurt me? All I did was drive through your shitty little town."

"Yeah and murdered a little girl you stupid cunt!" The girl screamed.

"I didn't mean to! She was going to give me away and you crazy bitches were already chasing me."

"It don't fuckin' matter. We do what we do here and don't need no Goddamn reason. You should know, I'm Candi Jean. Remember that name when your ass is rotting in hell." Candi Jean said as she walked to the oven where there was a kettle of boiling water. She grabbed the kettle and walked back to the table. "If I pour this up your pussy, will you lay me a hardboiled egg?"

She began pouring the water along Isis' naked crotch. The boiling water sizzled against her skin as pain shot through her legs and her whole body. It felt as if someone was ripping her flesh from her bones. Crying out, she struggled against her bindings.

"I will fucking kill you, you little blonde bitch." Isis said through gritted teeth.

"I doubt that cunt. I might just leave you all fucked up instead of killing you just to hear you whimper," Candi

Jean said as poured more boiling water on her legs, and running it all along her stomach and chest. Isis closed her eyes and tried to imagine she was somewhere else. When she was in her teens, her mom's boyfriend used to abuse and torture her regularly.

His name was Ariel, she'll never forget that asshole. His creepy, toothless smile as he'd hold her down by the throat, choking her while sticking his dick in her pussy and tearing her open. It hurt like hell, but it was the humiliation that made it even worse. She could handle the pain. Though there were times she barely handled it. The scars on her legs were from the beatings he gave her with his belt. There were burns on her back from Ariel branding her with a hot fireplace poker. Yes, she knew pain all too well.

Apparently her self-hypnosis was working as Candi Jean stopped with the hot water.

"What the fuck is wrong with you bitch? You're not even screaming," Candi Jean said.

"Maybe you're the one who is too much of a little

bitch to hurt me."

Candi Jean grabbed a meat tenderizer from the counter and smashed Isis' fingers on her left hand, repeatedly. Her bones crunched as they poked and jutted out of her fingers in all different directions. Isis bit her lip, holding in as much of her scream as possible. No way was she about to let this bitch get the satisfaction of her pain.

Candi Jean stood glaring at Isis. She could tell the redneck girl was getting pissed. Good. They'd never seen the likes of her around here that was for sure. They were probably used to suckering in families and college kids to fuck with. She was light years from any of those people. April had been pretty tough, but that old cowboy guy took her somewhere.

"You want to play tough bitch? Fine. I got no problem skinnin' you alive."

"Go for it. I don't think you can do it."

Candi Jean laughed at the challenge.

"Wow, you are gonna get it. Holy fuck. You have no idea. You will be begging me to kill you in a few minutes. You hear me. BEGGING!"

Isis began laughing hysterically as Candi Jean looked on, her face turning various shades of red.

"What the hell are you laughin' at bitch?" Candi Jean asked.

"You! Your face! Oh my god. You're trying so hard to act tough, but you fucking suck at it!" Isis said as she continued laughing to the point she was coughing.

"Shut up!" Candi Jean screamed, but Isis kept on laughing. "I said shut the fuck up!" She swung the tenderizer, striking Isis in the forehead. The blow stunned her, long enough to make her stop laughing. However as stars danced about before her eyes, she began to wiggle her broken hand against the restraint. Her broken fingers were now hanging loosely from her hand, allowing it to slowly work through the straps.

Candi Jean could see none of this however as she gloated over her newly asserted authority.

"I knew what would shut you the fuck up. Next time, I'll knock your fuckin' teeth in."

Isis resumed laughing, however only angering Candi Jean further as she raised up the meat tenderizer again.

"I'm warning you! Shut the fuck up!"

Isis kept laughing as Candi Jean brought it down one more time. This time, Isis blocked it with her free wrist, which stunned Candi Jean. Isis knocked the tenderizer away as she fumbled with freeing her other hand. Candi Jean punched her in the stomach, which briefly knocked the wind out of her. Frantically she worked at the buckle to free other heathy hand. Doing so was difficult with throbbing, broken fingers, but she managed just enough to free herself.

As Candi Jean bent down and picked up the meat tenderizer and came up with it, Isis grabbed it from her hand and blasted the side of Candi Jean's head, knocking her to the floor. Isis reached up with her good hand and undid the straps around her head and neck as she sat up and finished freeing herself.

She jumped off the table as Candi Jean was slowly getting to her feet. Isis ran to the sink and grabbed a frying pan, reared back as if she were Babe Ruth and smashed Candi Jean in the face. The blonde went sprawling onto her back as Isis dropped to a knee with the pan and smashed her again in the head. She then turned the pan to its side and struck Candi Jean on the top of the head with the edge. Over and over she swung as Candi Jean screamed and grunted with each blow.

After almost a dozen strikes, her skull gave way and caved in as she continued her barrage. Blood sprayed everywhere as Candi Jean's face imploded. Isis screamed with each blow until Candi Jean's head was nothing more than a pulpy pile of blood and mush. Isis stood and tossed the pan to the side staring down at the body. She didn't even feel her broken hand anymore as adrenaline coursed through her. When she caught her breath, she looked around and headed outside. It was time to leave this rat fuck town.

Chapter 10

April awoke in what looked like a hospital room. The bed was clean, warm and comfortable. As she sat up and pulled the blankets back, she saw her clothes were gone once again and replaced with a thin gown. In the past year or so, she had little to no modesty when it came to clothing. Seems everywhere she went she ended up naked.

She climbed out of the bed and walked to the sink looking in the mirror. Someone had cleaned her up, though she still had some scratches on her face and arms. There was a closet in the room, but it was empty. Walking over to the door, she pushed on it, only to find it locked. She pushed, pulled and even kicked it, but it was clear wherever she was, it wasn't a hospital.

The last thing she remembered was some old cowboy guy blasting some loud horn at her. She felt tired and groggy as if she'd been drugged. That's twice she'd been roofied in that fucking town. Assholes. She jumped as the door opened up and a small man with glasses and curly hair stepped inside. He was wearing a lab coat and had a stethoscope around his neck.

"Hello April. I see you're awake."

"Who the fuck are you?" She asked.

"I'm Doctor Cassidy. I'm in charge of your treatment."

"Treatment? Treatment for what? I'm not sick."

"Have a seat April," he said pointing to a chair. She stood glaring at him. "Please."

She reluctantly walked over and sat down as he sat across from her.

"April. I'm sure you realize this. You're a very special girl. I've never seen anyone quite like you."

"I would hope not," she said.

"Do you know what you are? Who you are? I'm sure you know what you can do."

"Yeah, I guess so. I know what I can do. Just did it by accident that one day. It was after I fell in that weird swamp in Browneye."

"Yes, but the swamp had nothing to do with it. If anything it was just a trigger," Dr. Cassidy said.

"Trigger?"

"Ok. People like you, or similar are called neuropaths, or neuros. You can exercise various forms of mind control. Yours is coupled with a sexual component and limited to men. Yet you have total control, it's really quite amazing."

"I'm glad you're impressed. Can I go now?"

"I'm afraid it's not quite that simple."

"Sure it is. You hand me my clothes, and I leave."

"We have some work to do, you as well. There is a lot we can learn from you. So unfortunately until we've done that, you'll have to stay here. I promise we'll make you as comfortable as possible."

"Yeah. That doesn't work for me," she said as she began thinking of what she could do to him. After a minute though, nothing happened.

"Your ability won't work. We injected you with an inhibitor, just as a precaution."

"Inhibitor?"

"All neuros have a common protein in their blood the rest of us don't have. We aren't sure why or where it comes from, it's the only common link we've found. So we have developed a formula that temporarily suppresses the protein, and limiting your ability. That way you don't make me ejaculate in my pants and force me to do something dangerous."

April was seething. She was getting sick of being drugged with shit, and now they rendered her helpless, whoever "they" were.

"Who the fuck are you people?"

"We're part of a special research company. Don't worry, who we are isn't the most important. You are what is important, April. You are making a huge contribution to humanity. Who knows what kind of diseases we can cure or treat after working with you?"

"I'm not a fucking guinea pig. I have rights. You can't keep me here."

"I'm afraid we can. Please lower your voice. Getting upset won't fix anything. There is no way out of here."

Without a word, April launched herself out of her chair and knocked the doctor onto the floor. She grabbed a pen from his coat pocket and put it to his throat.

"All right fucker, we're walking out of here," she said.

He remained extremely calm though as she pressed the pen against his throat.

"You don't want to do this," he said.

"The fuck I don't."

There were footsteps coming through the door. As she looked up, two large men in black uniforms ran into the room. One held out a cattle prod and pressed it against her chest and activated it. As electricity poured through her, April's body seized up as she collapsed to the ground. She wanted to fight, to stand up and punch these assholes, but was unable to move. The men picked her up and placed her onto the bed, but this time strapped her down using the soft restraints in each corner. Once she was strapped down, feeling began returning to her extremities but she was unable to move. Doctor Cassidy stood, put his glasses on and adjusted his coat as he looked at her.

"See April? Fighting us is pointless. You can be quite comfortable here if you just cooperate. Or you can fight and act like a lunatic, but you can see right now where that gets you," he explained.

"I don't want to cooperate. I want to go home."

"I already told you that isn't possible. You're in a situation you cannot control or manipulate. You can either keep fighting and be miserable, or make the most of it. The choice is yours." He turned and walked out of the room. Before he closed the door, he turned off the lights leaving her in total darkness. As she lie there, she stopped struggling and stared up at the darkness. She'd wanted out of Happytown, but this was not what she had in mind.

Chapter 11

Isis ran through the dark streets looking for a way out of town. She'd been able to find some clothes in the house after she killed that crazy Candi Jean chick. The bitches in this town were all fucking insane. She also grabbed a gun from the bedroom as she headed out. It was a little 9mm semi-automatic which fit perfectly in her hand. She grabbed a few extra magazines and shoved them in her pockets as well. Now she was sneaking through the streets, using the shadows as her cover, trying to find a way out.

There were a few cars parked in some driveways, but she was going to have to go after someone for their keys. There was no other way around it. One home had the lights on as she crept up and glanced through the window. This was a woman watching TV with two kids, a boy and a girl. The kids looked maybe eight or nine each. The mom looked to be in her thirties, maybe older. Not that any of that mattered.

Isis snuck around the back of the house and tried the back door. It was open as she slowly opened the screen door and crept inside, entering through the kitchen. As she guided the door shut, the mom came walking into the kitchen.

"You're that girl!" The woman said. Though Isis figured she meant that girl they'd been chasing as the whole town was nothing but girls. Without hesitation, she pointed the gun at the woman's face.

"Damn right bitch. Now let's go in the living room," she said.

"Look! I wasn't one of the ones chasing you. I don't have anything to do with that crazy stuff in this town. I just want to raise my kids. Please don't hurt us."

"Well if that's true, shut the fuck up and do exactly what I tell you. Now move."

They walked into the room as the kids both saw Isis and the boy jumped up on the couch.

"Mommy!" He screamed. "That's the bad lady! It's

her! Kill her mommy! Kill her!"

"It's ok, Christopher, just sit down please," the woman said.

"Not part of this town's crazy stuff huh? Kid's what? Seven telling you to kill the bad lady?"

"It's just what he hears. I promise!"

Isis pointed the gun at the boy, less than an inch from his face and pulled the trigger. The boy's head exploded as the gun blast rang through the house. His tiny body crumpled to the floor as his brains and blood painted the wall behind him. The little girl and woman both screamed. The women stepped forward to hold her son's body, but Isis wasn't having it.

"Back the fuck off bitch."

"My baby! You killed my baby! Why? Why?"

She pointed the gun at the little girl who was screaming.

"If you don't want your little girl to paint the walls you

better both shut the fuck up."

"Heidi, shhh! It's ok honey. Please," the woman pleaded with the little girl. "Please let me hold her, she'll quiet down faster."

Isis nodded as the woman grabbed the little girl and picked her up, holding her tight.

"Its ok sweetie, it'll be ok. She's not a bad woman. She's just scared ok. Just need to help her and we'll be ok."

"Christopher is dead! She killed him!"

"I know. I'm sorry. I really am." The woman was doing her best to stay calm, but Isis could tell she was about to lose it.

"Ok, enough mommy time. Where are your car keys?"

"They're in my purse."

"Bring it to me."

The woman walked over to a table and grabbed her purse, she opened it up, sliding her hand inside.

"Stop," Isis ordered. "Hand it to me."

She did as instructed as Isis sat it on the couch, reached in and pulled out the keys. Tossing them to the woman as she grabbed the little girl's hand.

"Come on. We're going for a ride."

"To where? You can have the car. Just take it and go."

"Not that simple. I need you two as insurance in case anyone decides to fuck with me. As you've seen, I don't give a shit if you're forty, or four. I'll fucking kill anyone who fucks with me. Now move."

They walked out to the driveway and into the sedan parked outside. Isis signaled for the woman to get in the driver's seat while he and Heidi climbed in back. The woman started the car and pulled out.

"Which way?" She asked.

"Whichever way takes us out of here. Try anything stupid and little Heidi here is dead. You understand?"

"Yes. Please, that's not necessary."

"What is your name unless you want me to keep calling you bitch?"

"Jill."

"Good Jill. Drive and get me out of here safely and you and your little rat just might live to see the sun rise."

Chapter 12

April awoke again, feeling groggy and dizzy. This time she was in an exam room, wearing sweats and a t-shirt. There was only an examination table she was sitting on as well as an empty counter nearby. There was no one else in the room, but there was a large mirror lining the far wall. She figured that was two-way glass, but wasn't sure why or what they'd be watching. Just for shits and giggles, she turned to the two-way glass and flipped the middle finger to whomever was watching.

After a few minutes the door burst open and security arrived with five men in handcuffs. The two guards wore black BDU's and some kind of riot helmets. The men they were escorting were all large, burly men. A couple looked like they could be bikers with their long hair, beards and tattoos. The other guys just looked like they were yanked out of prison. One of them had a shaved head and was covered in tattoos, including a teardrop on his cheek.

"Ok boys," the guard said as he uncuffed the men. "Play nice and have fun!" And they walked out, leaving her alone with them.

"What is all this?" April asked.

The men each circled around her, looking her up and down as if she were a side of filet mignon. One of them kept making some strange grunting sound as if he were playing pocket pool or something.

"Well, what do we have here?" One of the bikers said.

"They said we'd be getting recreation, but damn." Another said.

"Who the fuck are you guys? What's going on?" April asked.

"We're your party honey. And you're the party favor!"

One of the men grabbed her from behind, pulling her arms behind her. Another charged her, but she leaned back and kicked him in the stomach. The others rushed in grabbing her, tearing at her clothes.

"Stop it! Get the fuck off of me!" She screamed, but they continued pulling at her. They pushed her face down to the examination table, as several hands held her down. Someone began pulling at her sweats, ripping them off her legs, leaving her lower body naked.

"All right! Who's going first?" One of the men called out.

"I got this one. She is fine! I needs some of that fresh pussy!" Another said. She felt his hand on her ass as he thrust a finger inside her. It hurt like hell as he forced her lips apart, causing her to cry out.

"She's a screamer guys! This is gonna be a good one!"

Anger surged through her. Not just at her attackers, but with the assholes that were keeping her here, wherever "here" was. She was so sick and tired of being a victim, of people thinking she was there for someone's amusement, or sick games. Ever since she was kidnapped, it had been endless turmoil. She should have never gone on that road trip. If she made it out of here, she'd never leave the house again.

One of the men grabbed her by the back of the neck and shoved his dick in her face. She pinched her mouth shut as it rubbed against her nose and cheek.

"Open up bitch!" He shouted. "Time for breakfast!" He reared back and slapped her across the face, causing her ears to ring and the whole left side her face stung as it throbbed. He poked her in the face again with his dick.

"I told you to open up you fucking cunt!" He screamed as he reared back again for another blow. At the same time, the man behind her was pushing his dick up against her pussy, trying to force it in. The rage kept surging through April as she looked up at the man before her. He stopped and staggered backward as he grabbed his erect cock.

"What the hell? What is going on?" He yelled as the man behind her did the same thing. The others let go of her as they all doubled over yelling, moaning and gyrating on the floor. She wasn't sure how she was doing this with the inhibitor, but her ability seemed to be working. She ran over and pulled her sweats back on as the men twitched and gyrated as each of them climaxed. When they finished, they slowly stood looking around at each other.

April glanced at each of the as they all looked like deer caught in headlights.

"Now," she said. "Kill each other."

Without hesitating, yet still looking confused, the men all jumped each other and tumbled into a pile in the middle of the room. April climbed onto the table and sat cross legged as she watched one man gouge out another man's eyes as blood and fluid squirted out onto the floor. Another man strangled his foe, crushing his throat as the wounded man coughed and wheezed for air. Blood and bodily fluids oozed out onto the tile floor as the men did exactly what she was making them do. She had no idea how she' been able to break through, or why these guys were even there Most likely it was a test of some sort. She was little more than a lab rat to these assholes.

They continued struggling and fighting when the door burst open and more security was there. One of them had a big sound blaster like the cowboy in the cabin had.

Before she could react, it was on full blast, causing her ears to throb as she fell to her knees. The men collapsed as well as the guards ran in and despite her struggles, one of they gave her an injection. She got the easy end. One of the guards took out a gun and shot each of the men who had just attacked her moments before. April struggled against the drug, but it was useless. Her limbs grew heavy as her vision began to fade. Within a matter of seconds, sleep took her.

Chapter 13

Isis felt a huge sense of relief when they drove out of Happytown. The little girl sat crying and blubbering in the back seat. At least she'd stopped screaming. The girl's mother was whimpering from the driver's seat, but that didn't bother Isis as badly.

"So are you going to let us go now?" Jill asked.

"We got a ways to go yet. I need to get far far away from this place. Go south."

"Where are you wanting to go?"

"Mexico. Now shut up and drive."

For the next several hours they cruised along. The ride was mostly uneventful, and Heidi finally fell asleep. Isis was exhausted and felt like she could sleep herself. She wanted to, but couldn't' do it with these two. There was an exit up ahead as they drove into San Antonio. She tapped Jill on the shoulder.

"Pull off up here. We're going to crash for the night."

"We are? How will that work?"

"Just fucking do it," Isis said, pressing the gun into the woman's temple. Jill tensed as she pulled off the highway and into a hotel parking lot. It wasn't anything fancy, but wasn't a total dive either. Looking at the dash clock, it was just after two in the morning. She had to get rid of these two and keep moving south. "Pull around back," she ordered.

Jill did as she was told and parked near the back of the lot where Isis has commanded. There were no lights back there and no other car.

"Both of you, out," Isis said as she climbed out.

Isis got out and waved the gun at Jill who followed. She reached in and picked up Heidi who was sound asleep. Isis walked to the back of the car and popped the trunk.

"Get in. Both of you," she said.

"What? You're gonna make us sleep in the trunk?"

"Bitch, I am fucking tired of repeating myself to you. Get. In. The. Fucking. Trunk!"

Jill lay Heidi into the trunk and scooted her back and then she climbed in with her holding her in her arms.

"There. You got her good?" Isis asked.

"Yes."

"Ok. Hard to say when someone will find you guys."

"What do—"Before Jill could finish, Isis shot her twice in the face with a quick double tap. In an instant, there was nothing but a giant, gaping hole where her face used to be. Heidi jumped awake at the shot and began to scream, but Isis fired two shots into her as well and slammed the trunk closed. She really hadn't wanted to kill them. Part of her thought she could just leave them in the trunk and someone would find the later. But the more she thought about it, the more sense it made to them. No point in leaving witnesses or victims to run to the police. At least if she kills them it would buy her a few more hours at least.

Walking away, she tucked the gun into her waist band and walked around the front of the building. There was an eighteen wheeler parked in front of the hotel. The driver was an older man, well into his fifties wearing a t-shirt and Texas Rangers cap talking on a cell phone. He put the phone down when he saw Isis approaching.

"Well hello there," he said. "What's a cutie like you doing out this late?"

"Looking for a ride," she said putting an extra swish in her step as she approached.

"Well now. That would mean a lot of things."

"It just might."

"Where ya headed?"

"Mexico."

"Well, I'm headed to Laredo."

"That works too," she said. Laredo was right on the border, so she could cross from there or just lie low in Laredo for a while.

"Oh I might be able to get you there. What can you do for me?"

She walked up and ran a finger long his chest.

"I can do a lot for you."

Twenty minutes later they were in his hotel room. She never even asked the guy's name. He was naked, lying back on the bed as Isis road his cock repeatedly. She was impressed with how good of shape his body was for his age. His cock was even decent sized and functioned quite nicely. Her pussy throbbed as she slid up and down on him, as he stretched her out just enough to not hurt.

He lie flat on his back, his hands on her ass as she bounced up and down. Each time she came down, he thrust his hips upward and grunted. Finally he throbbed and stiffened inside her as they both climaxed together. Isis tensed and squealed as he filled her up. She continued writing, using her pussy to milk his cock dry. She took a deep breath and collapsed onto the bed at his side.

"Damn girl!" He said. "That was good shit. I haven't fucked like that in years."

"You weren't so bad yourself tough guy," Isis said. She climbed out of the bed and pulled her panties on.

"Where you going?"

"You mean we," she said.

"What in the hell are you talking about?" He asked.

"We are leaving for Laredo."

"You mean now? It's the middle of the night."

"Good! There won't be as much traffic," she said as she pulled on her jeans and shirt.

"Shit, I need to get some sleep."

"Fuck sleep."

"I'm not a kid like you girl. I'm old. My old ass needs rest."

"Tell you what." She climbed onto the bed with him and began massaging his cock through the sheets. "We leave now and you drive, while I give you as much head as you want along the way. Come on. You got to be lonely driving all the time alone."

"Well, you sure do make a convincing argument."

"Of course I do. So get up." She grabbed his Rangers hat and shoved it onto his head as she stood. As he got dressed, he looked over at her.

"Why do I get the feeling like you're running from something or someone?" He asked.

"Does it matter? I suck good dick."

"Well since you put it that way."

Chapter 14

April awoke and was strapped to a chair, which was like a cross between a dentist's chair and an electric chair. There was a leather strap around her forehead with electrodes fastened to each of her temples. She struggled against the restraints as Doctor Cassidy walked in.

"Hi April. Having a rough time of it I see," he said without looking up from his clipboard.

"What is this shit? Why am I here like this?"

"Well, you didn't listen to me earlier and you went nuts. So we've had to take some extreme measures. Plus you showed resistance to the inhibitor."

"How?"

"Those bikers you manhandled. You were on the inhibitor. All those men were just pulled out of prison and brought here as a test for you. You passed, or failed depending on how you look at it."

"What the fuck is that supposed to mean?"

"You showed for some reason you can bypass the inhibitor. So we need to find out why," he explained.

"How about you go fuck yourself?" She said, struggling against the restraints.

"I'm afraid that isn't an option."

She calmed herself and focused her mind on Cassidy. He looked up from the clipboard and activated a device in his hand sending an electric shock through April's body. Her legs tensed and chest heaved as the current ripped through her. April's vision went blurry until it subsided, and Cassidy did it again, this time longer. Once he let up, the current went away and April relaxed but she was in a cold sweat as she gasped for air, trying to get her breath.

"There. See what happens when you try to control me? You get a bit of a shock."

"Fuck you," she said, still panting.

"You have a very filthy mouth don't you. That's

unfortunate. I tried to help you April. Tried to work with you. So now we have to do things the hard way."

The door opened and a group of people in surgical garb, one was pushing a cart loaded with instruments.

"What the hell is this?" April asked.

"This is our surgeon and his team. They're here to examine you."

"Examine me?"

"You're special, April. You're also dangerous. We need to know what makes you tick. Not just for us, but for the betterment of mankind. Think of the good we could do if we could find out what you are, learn how to harness it, control it, and…"

"Package and sell it?" She finished.

"If need be. I supposed you already know you won't survive this procedure. It involves the removal of your brain so we can study it, your organs and central nervous system. In there somewhere is the key to April."

The idea of death had never really bothered her, even all the times she'd faced it recently. But those times had all been putting up a fight, going down swinging. She did not want to go down here, strapped to a chair like a fucking lab rat. They'd just put her to sleep, start cutting on her and she'd never wake up. She'd just be gone, forever. She hadn't spoken to her dad since weeks before the trip that landed them in Happytown.

"You're fucking murderers. You're not doctors, none of you are. My dad is an FBI agent. He won't stand for this shit. He'll find out what you did."

"You're right," Dr. Cassidy said. "He will." Cassidy walked over to the doorway and pushed open the door. He leaned out and stepped back inside. One man followed him in, it was the old cowboy that had brought her to this hell. Behind him, was her father.

"Daddy?" She whimpered.

"Oh my God. Baby," he said as he rushed to her side and knelt down.

"Daddy? What's going on? What is this place? They

want to kill me."

"I know. It's complicated. Grant here used to be in the Bureau with me years ago. He'd been reassigned and I never saw him again until the other day. I had no idea you were here or that this place even existed. Grant called me and explained you were here. I knew you were special April. I always have. I just had no idea how much."

"But the swamp at Browneye, that's when I was able to do this."

"That was just coincidence. Your grandma was a neuro. Not as strong as you, not by any stretch. I never knew what it was. When I was in high school some men came and took her away. They said she was sick. That was the last any of us had seen of her. My dad didn't want to talk about it. He looked scared to talk about it. Except a couple years later he said she died in a mental hospital. That was it. It was hard to deal with, but I just went along with it. Guess I was cut out to be a Fed huh? Just buy the bullshit and do what I'm told."

"Daddy, don't let them kill me, please!"

"I'm trying pumpkin, please believe me. These guys don't answer to anyone. Not even the president. They are scary as shit and afraid of no one. I'll do my best, I promise."

"Daddy, they're about to cut me open. They're going to remove my brain and study it."

"I know honey, I won't let them. I promise."

"Please?"

"Come on Bobby, it's time." Grant said.

"You can't do this. I can't let you kill my daughter."

"I reached out to you as a courtesy. So you could tell her goodbye. Most don't even get that. I promise you she'll go peacefully."

"No. This can't be happening. This is my daughter!" Bobby reached out and began to undo April's straps. Grant grabbed him as several other security guards also grabbed him, picked him up and carried him out the door. He kicked and screamed reaching his hand out to her. "April!" he cried as the door slammed shut in his face. She cried and sobbed as the hopelessness of what was about to happen sank in.

In just a few minutes, April Kennedy would be dead, gone, cease to exist. And there was nothing she could do about it. She didn't even struggle when they inserted the first needle. She just closed her eyes as the burn of the medicine pumped into her veins.

Chapter 15

Isis looked out the window of the truck's cab as they sped down the highway. The driver, who said his name was Hal. He hadn't stopped smiling since they left the hotel. She was starting to think he'd fallen in love. That was ok for the moment. Better the odds of him doing what she said.

"We need to get gas," he said. "Before we get on the freeway and out of town."

"Fine, just pick a place."

He pulled off an exit ramp and drove along the access road until they were at a twenty-four hour convenience store. He pulled the truck up to the diesel pump as Isis jumped out.

"I'm gonna get some cigarettes," she said.

He nodded as she ran inside. Once inside, she was shocked at how many people were in the store. It was just past four-thirty in the morning and it wasn't full, but there were far more than she expected. As she went to the cooler to remove a diet soda, a woman shoved her out of the way and grabbed on. She looked at Isis and shrugged.

"Sorry," the woman said and walked to the counter. Isis' blood boiled at the stupid cunt thinking she was just going to walk up and push her out of the way over a fucking soda. Isis grabbed her soda and walked to the counter. There the woman was in front of her talking to a man, she assumed was the woman's boyfriend. Each of the glanced back at her as the woman snickered. Keep it together. You already got cops on your ass and got a good head start. No need to stir shit up even more. But this fucking bitch and her boyfriend.

"You got a problem?" The snickering woman said.

"Maybe," Isis replied.

"Well take it somewhere else, and quit staring at me unless you want to fuck or something."

Her boyfriend, a chubby guy with a shaved head and hoop earring laughed.

"Aw damn baby! She couldn't handle you! Haha." He looked at Isis. "Sorry girl. My girl's pussy is gold!" He laughed again, exposing a cheap grille on his teeth.

Isis looked away and took a deep breath.

"Yeah, that's what I thought bitch, you better look away." The woman said. Isis wasn't even sure what happened then. It was as if something took over her body, something out of her control. Not unlike when she ended her boyfriend the other day. The rage hits and becomes a force unto its own. She wonder if that was what it was like to be possessed.

While everything probably only took a few seconds, it all went in slow motion as it was occurring. Isis pulled the gun out of her waistband and stuck it in the woman's face. The woman just froze as her eyes widened and she began to scream. Isis pulled the trigger firing the bullet into the woman's mouth and out the back of her head. The round exited her skull and also struck the old man behind her.

She then turned the gun onto the boyfriend and shot

him in between the eyes. The top of his head exploded as his body collapsed on top of his dead girlfriend. The other customers finally began to realize what was happening. Isis turned and shot the clerk twice, then spun and killed the old couple at the counter. There was a man at the ATM in the corner. He turned and put his hands up with tears in his eyes as he cowered on his knees.

"Please, don't hurt me! I didn't see anything! I won't say anything! I can't die! Please?" He pleaded, but she shot him twice in the chest as he buckled over. Two more people, a couple, had run out the door into the parking lot. Isis ran after them, one was already in a car while the other was trying to open the door. She quickly reloaded the gun and chambered a round, ran in front of the car and opened fire, shooting the man in the driver's seat six or seven times. Blood splatted onto the broken windshield as his body twitched with each shot. The women on the passenger's side turned and ran again. Isis ran up behind her and shot her in the back. The woman fell to her face as Isis stood over her and shot her four times in the back of the head. The fourth shot split the woman's head wide open, spilling its gooey gray contents onto the pavement.

Looking up, Hal was standing just a few feet away, his mouth gaping open.

"You fill up?" She asked, but he stood there looking lost. "I said did you get filled up?"

"Uh, yeah. I guess."

"Get in the truck. We gotta go!"

Hal stood in the parking lot staring at the carnage. If he didn't snap out of it, she'd need to shoot him too and she wasn't ready to do that just yet.

"Let's go!" She screamed as he turned and ran to the truck and climbed into the cab. He gunned it as they pulled out of the parking lot and back onto the access road and onto the highway as sirens wailed in the distance.

"Jesus fuck! You killed those people!" He screamed

"I know. Never did get my cigarettes."

"What? Cigarettes? What the fuck? Why did you do

that? Why did you kill them?"

"Some bitch pissed me off and her boyfriend was talking shit, so I shot them. Then I couldn't hardly just walk out of there, so I shot everyone else."

"Holy shit. I had sex with a serial killer. Fuck! You killed anyone else?"

"Yeah right before I met you. I killed some kid and her mom and stuffed them in my trunk."

"Jesus. Are you going to kill me?"

She reached up and touched the side of his face and smiled.

"Of course not Hal. I like you. Consider this a totally badass first date."

Chapter 16

April was asleep, but dreaming. In her dream, she was running through a field as a giant saw blade chased after her. No matter how fast she ran the blade got closer and closer. There was a barn just up ahead, but no matter how many more steps she took, it seemed further away. The saw buzzed louder and louder behind her as she strained to run away.

She tripped over a rock, landing on her face. Rolling over, she looked up to see the saw getting closer and closer. The huge blade screaming as it buzzed toward her, the smell of metal and oil burning her nostrils. Holding out her hand she screamed as loud as she could.

"No!"

Her eyes shot open and she was back in the dentists' chair from hell surrounded by the surgical team. One masked surgical tech stood inches from her with the bone saw just above her forehead. The women was motionless as the saw buzzed away. The woman's eyes darted from

April, to the doctor and other team members who looked on, confused. It took April a moment to realize what was happening.

April's gazed burned into the woman's eyes. The woman's eyes went wide as a tear began running down her cheek, the reality of what was happening finally hitting her.

"Kill them," April said.

Immediately the woman spun around and cut through the surgeon's throat with the saw, blood and tissue glopped into all directions. The other staff screamed as the woman spun and sliced through one of her colleague's skulls. Another woman on the team ran to the door when April got her. Still stuck to the chair, April reached out with her mind, causing the woman to freeze. Just like with men, this one buckled over, moaning, and panting until she was in the throes of orgasm. Once she finished she stood and walked back over to the woman with the saw. She was also crying.

"Please don't do this," her new victim pleaded. "We

were only doing our jobs. I have a little girl at home."

"So your life is worth more than mine? I'm special and have no kids so I'm just a lab rat?" April said.

"It wasn't my decision, I just do what I'm told."

"Yes you do, and so does she," April said as the woman with the saw began slicing into the woman's skull. She screamed as the saw cut through her skull, the smell of burning hair, flesh and bone filled the room. Once the saw reached her brain, she twitched and gyrated in a weird seizure before collapsing to the ground.

The woman with the saw looked over at April.

"Let me out of this thing," April ordered.

The woman dropped the saw, walked over to April and began working her straps around her hands, feet, chest and head until she was free.

"You made me kill all those people." The woman whimpered.

"Yep. You were inches from killing me, so we are just

getting started sweetie," April said.

"Are you going to kill me too?"

"Yes, when I'm done with you. You're going to take me out of here. Let's go."

They walked out of the room and down the hall. The woman walked along side April as they wound through.

"Which way to get out of here. Lie to me and I will make you rip your own eyes out of your head. Do you understand?"

"Yes. Right this way. There's an elevator." They walked until they were at the elevator. A couple security guards were in front of the elevator wearing their black BDU's. One of them saw April, but she had seen them first. Both men doubled over, grunting as they ejaculated. Once they were done, April pushed the "down" button on the elevator.

"Rip your own throats out," April said. Her prisoner watched in horror as each man dug his fingers into his neck, screaming and thrashing as they fought against themselves, shrieking in pain as their fingernails tore through their own skin and muscle. He wrapped his fingers around his windpipe and pulled, tearing it away from his neck. There was a wheezing sound of the air escaping as his body kicked and thrashed for almost a minute then lie still.

The other guard was still digging at his neck, but April got onto the elevator and pulled the woman on with her and hit the button for the ground floor. Looking at the elevator numbers, she saw they were on the eighteenth floor. The woman looked at April as the elevator went downward.

"How do you do that?" She asked.

"Do what?"

"That thing. Control people's minds, make them come. What the hell is that?"

"I don't know. You didn't come did you?"

"No. I guess not."

"I have no idea. I just think about it and it happens.

Never worked on girls before until now."

"I'm really scared. I don't want to die."

"Neither do I. Don't worry. Don't give me any shit, and I'll make it quick."

The doors popped open and April stepped into the lobby of some kind of corporation. She thought they were in some kind of hospital. There was a huge logo that said "Jericho Systems" with a huge desk at the front with a young, attractive blonde sitting behind. People were milling about and there was a huge fountain along the far wall.

"What the fuck is this place?"

"Jericho Systems. We're a research and development firm."

"I thought this was some hospital."

"You were on one of our medical floors where we do…" her voice trailed off.

"Do what?"

"Animal testing."

"God, you people are unfucking believable. Who was that guy that brought me here? And where did my dad go?" April asked.

"He's Grant Storm, one of our trackers. He goes after people like you...neuros. Normally they don't bring them in, they just kill them. They brought you in because you're special. Stronger. Guess you're stronger than any of us thought."

"Guess so."

A man in a suit wearing a security badge walked over to them. The girl was still in her surgical scrubs while April was only wearing a torn up t-shirt and a pair of shorts.

"Is there a problem ladies? Everything ok?" The man asked. He was tall and muscular with a shaved head. He was looking to the girl since she obviously worked there. Her eyes darted to April and then back at the man.

"We're fine thank you. Everything is fine," the woman

said. He nodded and began to walk away when the walkie-talkie in his hand chirped.

"All departments. 1270 in research level. Repeat 1270 on research level. Lock down all areas."

The man turned, looked at April then shouted.

"Emergency lockdown now! Lock it down!" People began screaming as he pulled his gun and trained it onto April, she was too quick though using her mind to make the woman jump in front of him as he opened fire. The rounds struck the girl several times in the chest as April dove out of the way and seized onto him causing him to double over as he grabbed his crotch, moaning and grunting. Other's came at her, not taking any chances in seconds everyone on the lobby was lying on the ground writhing in the throes of orgasm.

April bent down and dug through the security man's jacket until she came up with a set of keys. She stood and ran toward the door. Gunshots rang out around her. Turning around she saw Grant Storm standing by the elevator with his gun out shooting at her. Her father wasn't with him, so no telling where he may have gone. She used her mind to force the downed security guard to his feet and jump on Storm. She tried to reach into his mind, but it was like something was blocking her.

As the two me tussled she ran out of the building and into the parking garage. Using the keyless remote she ran in between the cars until she heard the doors chirp. The car was a black sedan. She climbed in, started it and peeled out of the garage and onto the city street. She recognized that she was in downtown San Antonio.

For some reason, she figured she was once again in the middle of nowhere. She had no idea where to go and calling her dad was out. Her first priority was to disappear into the early morning traffic. Though she'd have to come back later and destroy this evil place.

Chapter 17

Grant ran to the door way, and watched as April drove off. Looking around the lobby, people were just recovering from their April-inflicted orgasms. He wasn't sure what happened, but the girl got stronger all of a sudden. Funny thing was, as much as he killed neuros over the years, he had to admit he was pissed he went to all that trouble just so they could cut her open and study her. Once again, despite all their precautions, it hadn't been enough.

Jesus, they had her under anesthesia and she still took over, and had graduated to controlling women on top of it. The surgical room was a complete bloodbath. Seems once she learned a new aspect of her ability the girl didn't waste any time. She had to be put down though, the little beauty was a killing machine pure and simple. He'd never seen anyone like her. Fortunately he got to the lobby just in time. Had he been sooner, she'd have had him.

He walked out to his truck and climbed inside. As he

fired up the truck, he turned on the police scanner. Grant had no idea where April would be headed, but had no doubt she'd be generating some kind of police radio traffic real soon. After a few minutes, his phone began to ring.

"Storm," he answered.

"What the hell happened?" Bobby Kennedy, April's father asked from the other end.

"She got away. I guess she snapped awake before they operated. Weren't you trying to keep her alive?"

"Yes, but not to kill the entire surgical team and take off."

"Well, she's your kid. Any idea where she'd go?" Grant asked.

"I know she won't be calling me. She's totally on her own, no telling what she will do. I've seen her in action when cornered. It's scary."

"I know Bobby, isn't that why you came to me to begin with?"

"I wanted to protect her and others. What happened to your fucking inhibitor?"

"It didn't work as well on her as we'd hoped. It did at first, but she overpowered it. Your little girl is no joke Bobby, she's a tough chick, and scary."

"Can you get her back?"

"I think so."

"Alive?"

"No promises. I'm not going to put myself at risk over some fuckin' neuro. Not even your daughter."

"Shit."

"Yeah I know. I'm going to keep an ear out. She'll turn up soon. I don't doubt that."

Grant hung up the phone as a tone went out over the scanner. It was a call about a mass homicide at a local convenience store, at least seven dead, maybe more. Well that sure didn't take long. He fired up the pickup and headed to the address listed. It took him about twenty minutes to arrive. The place already had police cars swarmed around it with crime scene tape stretched around the outside and the parking lot. He climbed out of the truck and approached, holding up his badge.

"Texas Rangers," he said as he ducked the tape and walked in, surveying the scene. There were several bodies outside lying on the ground and covered with sheets. Inside there were several more but uncovered. One officer approached him.

"Fucking mess isn't it?" The officer said.

"So what happened here? Any idea?" Grant asked.

"I guess two women got in an argument, and one started shooting but decided to kill everyone."

"Jesus Christ. Slight overreaction."

"You can say that."

"Did the camera catch anything?"

"Yeah, they're in back reviewing it right now. Right this way." The officer said. Grant followed him to the back office were a couple detectives were around the monitor. Grant stepped in to take a look. They were just at the part where the shooting begun. Grant took a closer look and saw the girl's face. Son of a bitch. It was the girl who'd been with April in Happytown. He could have taken her out too, but that wasn't his job at the time. Not like he knew she as a homicidal psycho at the time anyway. Regardless, it wasn't April, though it didn't sit well with him this nut was in town also. Would just make his job harder with the cops even more on edge.

He slipped out the back and circled back around to his truck. Once he was in he headed back to the highway and toward downtown. He had a feeling April would stick to the densely populated parts of town, like downtown or maybe the parks. Somewhere it would be harder for him or others from the organization to make a scene. Though he'd done takedowns in the middle of supermarket, he was familiar with the thinking. Though April didn't think like other neuros, or anyone for that matter.

As he drove he thought about he and Bobby's conversation. It was true, Bobby had called him after she'd disappeared on the road trip. Happytown was a bizarre place with one of those mysterious Funhouses. Bobby was familiar with them too. Grant didn't know much about them other than the feds tolerated them spread out in some tiny towns around the country. When Bobby heard what happened to this one, he knew it had to be April. He'd said they tried to fuck with her, which of course, that's what the Funhouses do. But in typical April fashion, she literally shredded everyone; with a chainsaw.

The girl was not afraid to get her hands dirty, that was for sure. Unlike most neuros, she wasn't just a puppet master, she was the whole damn show. Suddenly the scanner squawked to life. This time was a disturbance at The Alamo. The Alamo? They said a women in a skimpy shirt and shorts was giving security a hard time and assaulted several of them, but no one could subdue her. That's April. No idea why she's at The Alamo, but he headed that direction.

Most are familiar with the story of the Alamo and the huge standoff between the Texans and Mexican army in

1836. The Mexican army killed everyone there, including Davey Crockett. They were later capture or killed by Sam Houston and his men, but "Remember the Alamo" was a cry Texans still remembered.

Since that time, the rest of downtown San Antonio had sprung up around the old battle site. It looked quite strange really. You see this 1800's mission and across the street is a wax museum and a movie theatre. Inside the Alamo was mostly a gift shop along with a courtyard and some old displays. It was strictly a tourist attraction, so no telling what April was doing there and fighting with security. He would find out soon enough.

Chapter 18

"Hal, I like you dude, but you need to chill the fuck out," Isis said. They were on the south side of San Antonio having stopped at a little café. Hal wanted to keep going, but Isis insisted they stop for breakfast. Mass shootings made her extremely hungry for some reason. While she was sure no one had seen them, Hal seemed to think a cop was ready to jump out at them at every corner.

The dude was cute and had been fun to be around, but he was starting to piss her off. At this point, she really didn't care if the cops came for her. Granted she wanted to have as much fun as long as she could, but if the cops showed up for her, she is taking as many out as she can before they get to her.

"I'm sorry. This is just, I never killed anyone before," he said.

"You haven't. I have."

"Yes but I was your getaway car. That makes me an accessory!"

"Dude, no one saw you, they aren't coming for us, just fucking drop it ok? Have some fun. You got any weed?"

"No, I don't drive around with it."

"Shit. We need to get you some, get you to chill. If you don't, I'll have to fucking kill you."

"Shit."

"Hey. Let's go fuck some more in the back of your truck," she suggested.

"What? Now?"

"Hell yeah now. I'm pretty turned on from earlier. Talk about a rush."

"Jesus, you are a crazy bitch."

"Yep! You liked it before."

"That was before I knew you were a kill crazy psycho."

"Hey, don't judge. Let's go."

She stood and walked him to his rig while holding his hand. They climbed into the back where his cot was and she undid his pants. Reaching her hand down the front, she took out his cock and began stroking. He didn't get very hard at all. So she leaned in and inserted it into her mouth, sucking the tip while running her tongue all along his shaft, all while massaging his balls. Still nothing. Earlier he'd gotten rock hard. Now his dick was like a limp noodle.

"What the fuck is wrong? You don't like me all a sudden?" She asked.

"No, it's not that. I told you, I'm not used to this kind of crazy action. Shit. You gunned down all those people. So am I your hostage or what?"

"No honey, I told you I like you. You're fun."

"Can we just go our separate ways? I won't talk to the cops or anything."

"Oh Hal!" She said as she jumped off him and

climbed into the front seat. "You are such a fucking pussy. Just start the truck. Let's get out of here."

"You're not gonna let me go are you?"

"Just get my ass to Mexico. Then we'll talk about your future."

Without another word he started the truck and pulled out of the café's lot. She turned on the radio where she heard the first reports of her earlier shooting.

"You hear that shit? That's us! They're talking about us!"

"Yeah, and the cops and Texas Rangers and Feds are looking for us. Holy shit. I'm so fucking dead. We both are. You know that don't you."

She rolled her eyes, not entirely sure why she hadn't killed him already. As much of an annoying bitch as he was, there was something sweet about him too, but she knew at the rate he was going, it wouldn't be long. Though it didn't help matters when police lights appeared behind them.

"Shit! You see that? Shit! It's the cops!"

"Just chill. Maybe you were just speeding," she said.

"Hell no. There's six of them, all with their lights on. They know it's us. Shit. I'm not going to prison. I'm definitely not dying in prison."

"Just speed up," she said. "Quit driving so slow, and gun this thing."

"It's an eighteen-wheeler. I'm not gonna outrun a bunch of cops. Plus I'm sure they got a road block up ahead."

"Fucking gun it I said!" She screamed sticking the gun against the side of his head. He looked at her and stopped on the accelerator, shifting gear as the engine screamed while they picked up speed. The police cars sped up, one pulled up alongside them as Hal swerved, crowding the cop into the other lane. Sure enough way up ahead he saw a road block a big one. There was a SWAT truck and officers with shotgun and rifles lined up aiming at them.

"You see that! We're fucked!" He yelled.

Isis pressed the gun harder into his temple.

"Not as fucked as you'll be if you don't stop acting like such a pussy and drive!"

He glanced at her again, this time, grabbing the barrel of the gun and pressed it to his forehead and squeezed her finger.

"Hey!" She yelled right before the gun went off, splattering Hal's brains all over the driver's side window. Instantly the truck began to veer wildly along both lanes as the road block got closer. Police began opening fire on the truck as Isis grabbed the wheel trying to exercise some control over the rig, but Hal's dead body had flopped over the wheel as his foot pressed harder on the pedal, increasing their speed even more.

Gunshots bounced off the truck as some came through the windshield. Isis ducked as she felt the truck crashing through the roadblock, veering rapidly from side to side as the left side of the vehicle came off the ground. It jerked wildly to the right smashing through the guardrail and into a field where it landed on the passenger's side and slid to a halt. Isis was now lying on her side, she felt something in her side crack, she wasn't sure what it was, but it hurt like hell.

Hal's dead body was on top of her, pressing her against the window as she struggled to breath. She heard footsteps approaching and officers' shouting orders to each other as she looked around but the gun was lying by the gas pedal under Hal's feet. So much for going down in that blaze of glory.

Chapter 19

April couldn't believe it; of all the places to run out of gas, it had to be downtown right in front of the Alamo. She pulled the car to the edge of the street, and jumped out before some parking attendant yelled at her. The street across from the Alamo was lined with stores and tourist attractions. She ran across the street and figured she'd head inside the old mission for a while. At least there was a large crowd there and no one would attempt anything.

That and they'd expect her to be on the run, not sticking around nearby, though finding the car might tip them off. She hoped they'd be expecting her to get on a bus or something to get far away, not hang out under their noses. As she walked through Alamo Plaza, there were tour buses parked all over and packs of elderly people and school groups lined up to get inside.

She approached the main entrance and attempted to slip in unnoticed.

"Excuse me, ma'am you can't go in there," the doorman said. So much for unnoticed.

"Why not? There's no fee to get in."

"You're not wearing shoes."

For fucks sake.

"Yeah I was attacked earlier, I barely got away."

"So you came to the Alamo?"

"Fine, whatever." She said as she began to walk away.

"Hey beautiful, you need some help?" Some guy said from behind her. She was just a few feet from the Alamo when he ran up and grabbed her arm. He was older, maybe in his fifties, with super long hair and a beard, wearing a biker vest and board shorts. Strange ensemble or whatever.

"No, thank you. Just having a rough day. I'll be fine," she said as she tried to turn away, but he grabbed her arm again. "Could you not touch me please?"

"You wanna go grab some coffee or food or

something. There is a real nice place just down the street."

Now she was getting irritated. She looked and felt like shit, yet this guy was still hitting on her.

"No. Thank you. Now please let me leave."

"Wow, look you fucking bitch. I'm being real nice here. You look like you just got roughed up turning tricks and your skanky ass is going to be a bitch to me? Fuck you." He squeezed her arm tighter and began to drag her away.

"Let go of me!" She demanded.

"I'm going to teach you some fucking manners. Skanks like you are a dime a dozen. You don't get to talk to me this way."

"Seriously, you don't want to do this."

"Or what bitch? What're you going to do?"

Without answering, she did it, a bulge appeared in his shorts as he doubled over, grunting and moaning.

"What the fuck? What's happening?"

"You're mine now asshole." She said.

After a few minutes, the guy was gyrating as he ejaculated in his own shorts. As he lie there breathing heavy, he looked up at her scared and confused. April looked around and spotted a couple of San Antonio police officers standing on the corner talking.

"Go jump one of those cops, get his gun and then shoot the other one," she ordered.

He stood, trying to resist the order, but physically unable to.

"What's going on? I don't want to jump a cop! Why can't I stop myself?" He yelled as he ran to the officers. He tackled one of them and began struggling for his gun. The officer on the ground tried to fight the man off, but the man was too strong. The second officer tried to struggle with him as well, but the man got the gun away and jumped to his feet. The second officer drew his gun and fired, shooting April's attacker, killing him instantly.

The crowd around the Alamo began to scream and scurry around. Amid the commotion she ran inside toward the building, but another officer saw her running and took off after her. She burst through the door and into the hall of the old mission. People were screaming as more gunshots rang out from somewhere. So much for a low profile. She turned a corner and there was another cop with his Taser out. She stopped but he shot her, striking her between the breasts with the prongs the current coursed through her knocking her flat on her back.

The other officer ran up and handcuffed her. She could have used her ability on the cops, but they were already on high alert as it was, she didn't want to really set them off, nor did she want to actually hurt a police officer. Sending that asshole after them was just a way to get him shot. Besides, a few hours in jail, she could at least get a nap in and maybe something to eat. At lease she didn't think the assholes from that research place could get her there. Though when she was ready to leave, she could always just make them let her out.

"What's your hurry? I saw you fighting with that guy before he attacked my partner. Want to tell me what that was about?" The cop said as he pulled her to her feet.

"He burned my toast at breakfast this morning," April replied.

"Cute. Well you can cool off in a holding cell until we sort this out." As he walked her outside, she considered using her phone call to call her dad. Trouble was, she wasn't sure if her dad was still on her side. Why would he not tell her about being a neuro and his cowboy pal or maybe that people would want to kill her? It was too much to think about. She pushed the thought to the back of her mind as the officer shoved her into the back of his car and shut the door.

Chapter 20

Isis limped into the holding cell. There were two other women sitting in there, one of them looked really familiar.

"Don't I know you?" She said to April.

"Probably not," April answered.

"Yes I do. You're the chick from that crazy town. What the hell? That weird cowboy dude came and got you."

"Yeah that was rather fucked."

"What was that? Was he a cop?"

"Not exactly. Why are you here?" April asked.

"I killed some people."

"Some people?"

"Had a bit of an incident at a convenience store," Isis said.

"I bet. You're a crazy bitch."

"Whatever. So what are you in for?"

"Long story," April said.

Isis remembered April as being pretty, but sitting there against the wall she looked more beautiful, even though she was filthy and looked exhausted. Isis moved closer to her. They were the only two women in the cell for the time being. Isis wasn't sure why she was feeling turned on all of a sudden. She was fairly certain April wasn't doing her thing to her.

"Hey," Isis said. "Are you doing that thing to me?"

"What thing?"

"You know. That thing you do to people."

"No. Why?"

"I feel horny as hell for some reason."

Isis had only ever been with maybe two girls in her life. Both had been fun, but nothing to get overly excited over. She didn't consider herself bisexual though. It had been more of an experimental thing. Isis walked closer to April and leaned on the wall next to her.

"What?" April asked.

"You're really hot, you know that?" She said while stroking April's hair.

"Yeah. I do know."

She expected April to pull away, but the girl looked as if she needed the comfort. Hell, the girl was tied up naked in a barn when she'd found her. No telling what kind of horror she'd been through recently. Isis had been through plenty of her own. She knew that look when she saw it.

April turned and looked at her. The second her huge blue eyes locked in with Isis' gaze, her pussy was immediately drenched. There was something special about this girl, that much was certain.

Isis leaned in and kissed April on the lips. Much to her surprise, April returned the kiss. Isis put her hand on the back of April's head as they kissed deeply and passionately. Her hands sliding all up and down April's body as their breathing increased. April's body was firm, yet soft, and perfect in every way. As she worked her hands around, she slid her hand down April's shorts, and teased her clit.

April's blue eyes went wide, as she gasped with each flick of Isis' finger. Isis then slid two fingers inside of April who gasped as she continued kissing Isis. As her breathing picked up, April slid her hand up Isis' shorts as Isis felt her soft fingers slip inside of her. It felt so good. As April worked her fingers in and out of her, she couldn't help but wonder how many girls April had been with. They continued to finger each other, more intensely, faster and faster as they held each other close. Finally they both hit their climax together. As they calmed down, they sat there holding each other.

Isis pulled away and looked at April who for a moment looked confused, Isis was about to speak when the door slid open and the old cowboy stepped into the cell.

"Well look here," he said. "It's like we got a family reunion." He looked Isis up and down. "Hope I'm not interrupting anything." He nodded toward Isis. "Sounds like I should have taken care of you while I still had the chance."

"Well good thing you didn't I guess," Isis replied.

"You got some real balls coming here," April said. "How do you know I won't use my ability on you?"

"I figured you only got arrested because you wanted to. Trying anything on me here, sure you could. But would draw a lot of attention. Attention I know you don't want."

"So why are you here? You obviously got pull. You gonna kill me right here and say I killed myself?"

The cowboy laughed as Isis tried to figure out what they were talking about.

"Let's call this neutral turf for now, shall we? I wanted to tell you that things weren't supposed to go like that with you."

"Oh right, you were supposed to kill me there on the table."

"Look. Normally my job is to take out you people on site. I could have done that easily back at the cabin. But they said you're special or some shit."

"That's what I hear. So instead of just shooting me, you take me into be cut open like some lab rat. But hey! At least you brought my dad in to say goodbye. Is he the one who sold me out?" April asked.

"You're making this way too complicated. They just told me they wanted to run some tests. Here's the thing. I got a lot of pull around here. I'm going to get the paperwork around to have you transferred into my custody. Then we'll go from there."

"Why are you telling me this?"

"Like you said! You're special. I've been doing this job for thirty years. Gotten pretty damn good at it too. Too damn good. I need a challenge. Though catching you at the cabin was pretty easy. In all fairness you had no idea me or the company existed. Now you do. So it'll be more fun that way. So you got a few hours to take all that in." He stepped out of the cell and nodded to Isis.

"What the fuck was that all about?" Isis asked. "Special? What'd he mean by you're special?" Isis looked April up and down. Sure she was hot, but unless she had gold plated tits or a pussy made of platinum, there wasn't anything special about the bitch.

"Like I said, long story."

"You know, I'm trying to be nice to you bitch. I helped you back in that little fucked up town. I could have left you hanging."

"You're right. I'm sorry," April pulled her hair back and tied it into a ponytail. "Want to help each other out again?"

Isis' curiosity was piqued. If she didn't break out of jail, she'd get the needle for sure.

"Ok, help how?"

"I know a way out of here. I can make you help me if you want to or not. If you can keep it together, you can just help me out on your own and once we are out of here, you go back to whatever you were doing."

"Ok. Most of that made no sense. So what did you have in mind?"

"Give me a second," April said as she walked over to the cell door. There were several officers standing around the booking area, both male and female. She closed her eyes and in a matter of seconds, all of them had fallen to the ground, grabbing their crotches, writing and moaning until they each orgasmed. Isis watched in bizarre fascination.

"What in the actual fuck? Holy shit! Are you doing that?" Isis asked.

April didn't reply as several officers walked to the cell and opened the door, letting the girls out.

"Take us out of here," she said to them.

"I can't," the male guard said.

"You can and you will," April answered. He turned and began leading them out into a hallway.

"Fuck! What is wrong with me?" He yelled as he walked to a metal door and unlocked it.

"Just not your day boss," April said.

"He' cute. Can I keep him?" Isis asked.

"No. I don't kill for fun."

"Oh, all judgy now are we? You're like fucking Carrie except you mind rape people. I bet you've killed more people than me."

April grew quiet as they continued walking. Bingo. Isis figured her and this April chick will either be good friends, or she's gonna have to kill the bitch. Though she was an incredible lay. No guy or girl had ever made her come that hard. And that was hurried in a jail cell. Isis shuddered to think what they could do together alone in an actual bed. Either way Isis liked to enjoy the ride wherever it ended up. Though she was positive nothing about this series of events was going to end well for any of them.

After a few more turns, they were walking through the kitchen and out into a loading bay. The officer stood looking at them, terrified.

"They're going to put me in prison. They'll think I helped you escape," he said. April ignored him and put out her hand. "Car keys." She said.

He dug into his pocket and handed her a set of keys.

"Which one is it?"

"It's a red Prius."

"Are you fucking kidding me?" April said. "A Prius?"

"My wife wanted it. She's a Democrat."

"Whatever," April said as they turned and left him standing there.

Isis couldn't stop giggling.

"That's funny as shit. So you can like make people do whatever you want?"

"Something like that."

"That is fucking awesome! Can you teach me? Like how do you do it?"

The doors to the Prius chirped as they squeezed in to

the tiny car.

"I can't teach it. I just do it. Like I can't teach you to grow a dick. You either have it or you don't," April explained.

"Trippy. Where we going? I need to get to Mexico."

"Why Mexico?"

"It's not here."

"Good point. I need to make a stop first. You can have the car once I get there."

"What kind of stop?"

"I have to kill a bunch of bad people."

Chapter 21

April drove the Prius through the midday traffic. She kept hitting her head in the tiny car every time they moved or swerved. Isis seemed to be having way too good of a time as the car weaved through the streets until they arrived at Jericho Systems.

"So what are you doing here?"

"I'm going to kill these motherfuckers."

"You just gonna walk right in the front door and start wasting fuckers?" Isis asked. April glared at her as Isis nodded. "Oh, right. You're gonna do that to everyone in there?"

"Yep."

"What if some of them don't know what goes on there? You just gonna kill them too?"

April almost burst into laughter. The idea of Isis lecturing her on the morality of revenge killing was not even funny. The girl so far had just wasted people for no more than being in her way or talking shit, now she wanted to get all high and mighty on April.

Though Isis did have a point, and April was sure at some point all of the bloodshed in the past week will take its toll on her. So far, she hadn't had a minute to sit and reflect on it. It was hard on her after everything in Browneye, all the people she'd killed. After what she did to Happytown and what she was about to do would make that look like a day at the park.

There was always the option to not go into Jericho Systems and waste everyone, but the mere knowledge that they do what they do in plain sight in such a calculated and organized fashion made her blood boil. No, just no. Everyone working there was guilty. If they didn't know they should know. So fuck all of them.

"I don't really give a shit. They are all dying, and it's gonna hurt. A lot."

"You're a hard core bitch," Isis said.

April ignored her as they started walking inside. She

got to the door and realized Isis was behind her.

"What are you doing? Take the car and get out of here," April said.

"Hell no. I'm not missing this. You kidding?"

"Suit yourself," April said as she pushed the door open and stepped inside. There was a uniformed police officer inside talking to a man in a suit. Just hours before had been the shooting with the security guy. Looked like they were mostly cleaned up, so good timing on her part.

The woman at the desk gave April a strange look as she stood.

"Excuse me miss, aren't you that girl who…" she began, but April glared at her, instantly doubling the woman over into the orgasm. Even though she wasn't using her ability on Isis, the girl looked almost as turned on as the woman she was tormenting. A security guard walked over, but April turned her gaze at him, and in an instant, everyone in the lobby was once again erupting in their own bizarre world of sexual torments.

Isis ran over and grabbed the guard's gun and extra magazines, without hesitating she shot the guard in the face three times.

"Jesus! I was gonna use him!" April said.

"There's plenty more."

"Don't piss me of, you're not exempt here if you fuck with me." April said as she looked around at her new mind slaves.

"Get up every one! We're clearing this fucking building." They all stood looking scared and confused. April lead them to the stairwell where they headed to the second floor which was all offices. There were cubicles and larger offices there.

"What's going on here? You aren't cleared to be up here!" A man in a suit said who suddenly doubled over himself. He never got to finish his orgasm though as April ordered one of the women over to stab him in the throat with a letter opener. Blood oozed out as the man gurgled and gyrated on the floor. She shouted out commands to the rest of her minions who now numbered almost fifty.

Isis ran from office to office dragging people out. She bent one suited man who looked like he could be her grandpa over a desk and pulled his pants down, shoved the gun up his ass and fired. The bullet tore through is guts and ripped out his back. Even the ones under April's control became ill, some vomited right on the floor.

"Lick that shit up!" April ordered to one woman.

"Why? Why are you doing this?"

"You treat people like fucking animals! So you can see what it's like before you die. Fucking eat it!"

The woman tried to resist but she knelt onto the floor and began licking up her own vomit, though she gagged and threw up again halfway through.

"Eat it again and keep it down. I can do this all day. No one can fucking stop me. Do you understand? Do you know who has come for you today? You guys wanted to cut me open like some science project. Guess what, you fucked with the wrong bitch."

"Please!" Another said to her. "Most of us just do office stuff. I'm an accountant for God's sake! We don't even know what they do upstairs."

"Bullshit!" April said.

"Let's waste them all April!" Isis called out.

"Nah, they can waste each other."

In a few moments many of them were stripping naked and cutting, slashing and raping each other with various office supplies. The entire floor was filled with screaming and wailing as more security ran in from upstairs wearing their black BDU outfits. April immediately seized them with her mind. Each of them falling to the ground. She had them all strip off the baklavas they wore, she assumed to instill fear into their own employees as well as their test subjects.

After several more minutes of having her slaves rape and assault each other, the ones who could still walk were ordered up to the third floor.

"What about the ones who can't walk?" Isis asked.

"Kill them," April said as Isis opened fire on each of them. Isis stripped the MP-5's from the security guards and slung two of them over her shoulders as she shot one in the nuts just for fun. They got to the third floor which was extremely quiet.

After a quick search, a couple people were found hiding in offices and under desks. They weren't worth bothering with, so she had Isis shoot them each. The rest of the group were all crying and blubbering, the noise was giving her a headache.

"Shut the fuck up! All of you! Next person to cry, bitch or moan I'll have your coworker cut our asshole out and feed it to you!" She screamed.

The next several floors were also fairly dead. April figured people were all moving up to the higher floors which were more secure. That all changed when they got to the tenth floor. She was glad she'd had her slaves go through the stairs first. There were dozens of security guards waiting for them and opening fire, killing them and piling up bodies in the doorway.

April managed to reach out to them, taking control of all of them as well. This time there were some medical staff on the floor, most of whom tried to run, but to no avail. Among them was her old pal, Doctor Cassidy. He looked much less prim and proper since she'd last seen him. His hair was unkempt and clothes disheveled as she approached him shortly after causing him to jizz himself.

"April? I figured you'd be long gone," he said. "Why are you here?"

"What does it look like? I'm going to kill you all."

"Why? We were only trying to help you. I tried to help you."

"If that is your version of help doc, you are incredibly fucked up. Might want to re-read your Hippocratic Oath. I'm pretty sure it doesn't involve cutting people's brains out to be studied."

"Look, just let me explain!"

"No. No explaining needed." She said as she turned and pointed at a tall black man in a lab coat. "You," she said. "Come here and cut your own heart out."

"What?" He asked but helplessly moved toward her.

"Did I stutter asshole? Get the fuck over here and cut out your fucking heart. Doctor Cassidy is going to have some lunch."

The man sat down next to Cassidy, picked up a scalpel from one of the tables and began cutting into his own chest, screaming as he dug through the bone and flesh.

"Don't slip, I want to see how far you get before you die."

"Wow," Isis said. "I thought I was fucked up."

April really hated hearing Isis compare her to herself. As far as she was concerned they were nothing alike. April had her ability of course and there was a valid reason or every person she killed and how she killed them. Isis was just crazy. At least that is what April had been telling herself. The longer she watched her current prey digging his own heart out of his chest while be bled, cried and screamed, she began to wonder if she was completely losing her mind.

Chapter 22

Grant walked into the lobby after watching April and Isis come tearing through. He had to admit, this hadn't been where he'd expected them to go. Once he left the jail, he parked down the street waiting to see if she would attempt an escape, and sure enough she did. What he hadn't expected was for them to double back to Jericho and from what he saw just in the lobby, they had wreaked some havoc which was still ongoing.

Not to his surprise, his phone began to ring.

"Storm," he said.

"What the fuck is going on?" The man screamed. That man was Harold Cork, one of the wealthiest men in the country. Harold was also the biggest shareholder of Jericho Systems and its parent companies and subsidiaries.

"I figured she'd try to break out of jail. Instead she came back to Jericho and has killed a good share of them,

I think she's upstairs now finishing the job."

"Sounds like you're losing your touch, Grant. Years ago you'd have tagged and bagged someone like her. Now she's in our own fucking building?"

"Afraid so. I'm going to head up there now and kill her."

"You'll do no such thing. I already ordered the scorched earth protocol. Our tech guys are destroying all our data remotely. One of our operators on the top floor there will literally self-destruct the building in a few minutes, so I'd get out of there."

"Jesus, I didn't know you had a self-destruct protocol."

"We do for all our buildings. Explosive charges already in place. Just need the activation codes entered on site. First time we ever had to use one, so thanks for that."

"If you'd have let me kill her from the get-go this wouldn't be a problem," Grant said.

"I think you're forgetting who is paying you. You're also forgetting our lack of a retirement plan. So I'd mind my attitude."

"So what do you want me to do?"

"Get out of there and get to the Dallas location. We're having a meeting there with some other trackers after all this. I need you up there by tonight." Cork said as he hung up.

Grant looked around, he could hear screaming from the stairwell. No telling what was going on up there. He should just turn and leave. As many horrible things as Grant had done in his life, he hated to just leave all these people to die. There had to be hundreds in the building. Though he wasn't ready to die himself.

This was only the second time in his life Harold Cork had called him directly. The first time was when the old man ordered him to take out a fellow tracker while on an operation. They'd been hunting an entire gang of neuros holed up near Shreveport. The neuros were always way ahead of them no matter what they tried. Turned out, his partner whose name he couldn't even remember anymore. Wasn't that something? Turned out the guy was feeding the neuros their intelligence.

Apparently this guy's nephew was one of them. Somehow he managed to keep that information from the rest of the company. As a result, many trackers were killed and a lot of money was wasted. So one night they were parked a block away from where the neuros were thought to be hiding. Harold Cork himself called Grant and told him to take his partner out. So he did it. No hesitation, no second thoughts. He hadn't even hung up the phone. In a single motion, he raised his hand, pressed the gun to the man's head and pulled the trigger. They were on a first name basis then. To this day though, he couldn't recall what the guy's name was. Maybe he made himself forget. Not that it mattered.

Point being, Harold Cork didn't just call field operators at random and for no reason. In his case, he didn't want word to get out they had a traitor, so he played it close to the chest and made sure it was taken care of. Using that logic, and knowing this time he had blown this mission. Not only did they not get the samples and research they needed from the neuro, but she had gone on to kill an entire research center off. No, there wasn't going to be any big meeting in Dallas. The only meeting he had in Dallas was with the Reaper. There was no doubt in that.

So as far as Grant could tell, he had two choices. Go to Dallas and to certain death, turn around and leave for good, going into hiding. The third option is to see at least who he could save in this place before everyone died some horrible death. Running and hiding had never been his strong suit, nor had surrendering. So he drew his gun and headed for the stairwell. At least if he was going to die, it would be on his terms and putting up a fight.

Chapter 23

April didn't feel like herself anymore. She was starting to realize what she was, a mass murderer. Granted, everyone she'd killed had either been a murdering sociopath or someone who protected them, but the fact she had no trouble killing these people in the most disgusting ways she could imagine troubled her greatly. After she made the one doctor cut out his own heart until he collapsed, she made Doctor Cassidy eat it as if it were an apple.

It took him awhile, along with several breaks to throw up but he managed to get the whole thing down. Even April was impressed, though when Cassidy looked up at her, his mouth being smeared with red, bloody goo reminded her of those fucked up clowns in Happytown. Once he ate the heart, she was now watching several of the female staffers shoving various objects up his ass. His screams filled the halls as two girls held him down across a desk while two other jammed whatever they could find up there.

They'd already gotten a ruler, several pens and a sharpie in there.

"Come on, there's still room in there," April said. "

"Shouldn't we keep going? We have a few more floors yet," Isis warned.

April looked around before taking a deep breath. Isis was getting on her nerves, but she had a point.

"You're right. Finish him off."

Isis walked over and flipped one of the MP-5's off her shoulder and into her hands. She fired it at the group along the desk and giggled as their insides splattered against the wall. The doctor flopped off the desk and lie on the floor twitching. April shook her head as they headed up the next stair well. There were more security up there waiting for them. April took control of them easily enough as one man was in an office typing something frantically into a large computer terminal. She used her mind to double him over as he ejaculated all over himself.

A woman ran screaming out of an office from behind her carrying a large syringe. Before April could react, the woman tackled April, thrust it into her arm and pushed the plunger. Immediately April felt weak and woozy. Fuck! The inhibitor! She had no doubt that is what the lady injected her with, and it felt like a really high dosage too. At least, much higher than the ones she'd been previously given.

Isis gunned down the woman as April stumbled to her feet.

"You ok?" Isis asked.

"I'm not sure,"

"What the hell she stick you with?"

"It's this inhibitor. It's supposed to keep me from doing what I can do. These people were trying to cut me open earlier and study me like some biology experiment."

"That is fucked."

"Let's go see if anyone else is here," April said as they moved through the hall. They walked around each office checking doors until they reached the end of a hall and a large, steel double doors.

"What the fuck is this?" Isis asked.

"I have no idea."

There warning signs all up and down the doors that said "Warning" and "Caution" among other things. They were locked with no way to see what was in there. April turned to her group.

"Anyone know what is in there? Or how to get in?" April asked, but none of them answered. She rolled her eyes and looked at the group. "Ok, someone has about two fucking seconds to tell me how to get in this room and what is in here, or I'll make each of you scratch your own eyes out."

She looked as they all stared at each other, all looking horrified.

"One!" April called out, still nothing. "Two!"

"Wait!" A little old man in a lab coat came pushing his way to the front. "I work back there some times. It is where we keep our, um, specimens."

"Specimens? What the fuck does that mean?"

"Like projects that didn't go well or have the desired result. They may still have research value. So we keep them here," he explained.

"Open this fucking door," she ordered.

"I have to enter my passcode."

"Then get up here and do it!"

The little man walked up to the door and opened a panel along the wall, exposing a keypad. Reaching into his pocket, he pulled out a pair of glasses, unfolded them and placed them onto his face. He put them on and began punching in keys on the pad. After a few seconds, there was a hissing sound as the deadbolt on the large doors slid to the side, and the door popped open. April pushed it the rest of the way open and stepped inside.

There were men and women in lab coats who all looked as if they'd just been caught with their hands in a cookie jar. They froze in their tracks as April tried to take hold of their minds, but was unable with the recent injection of the inhibitor. It apparently didn't affect those she already had a hold of, but she couldn't control anyone new. She'd overcome the inhibitor before, but this was a huge dose. Her legs still felt weak and shaky.

Isis picked up on her difficulty though and just shot everyone in sight. She seemed to be enjoying her new toy. Though if she knew April was weak, she might try something. April didn't trust the girl at all, even as her own mind was fading toward the darkness. There were lots of weird sounds, like people crying and moaning. They walked past what looked like a nurse's station and past several rooms. The whole area looked like a hospital floor, more so than the area they'd held her earlier.

The moaning and crying got louder as they reached one of the rooms.

"What the fuck?" Isis said.

April saw it too and couldn't believe what she was seeing either. There on the bed was a human body strapped down. The body was wiggling and writhing except it didn't have a head. Well it did, but not attached. On a pedestal next to the bed, was the man's head, mounted on some kind of post. There was a series of wires and cables coming from the man's head and leading to his stump on his body. The man was looking down and crying, but it looked straight at April and its eyes lit up, showing something it probably hadn't felt in a long time. Hope.

"Help me! Please! You can help me!" The thing cried. It was a man, but somehow being kept alive. April looked at Isis who, for the first time since they'd been together, looked horrified.

Chapter 24

Grant walked through the hall and approached the corner. He heard some commotion up ahead. His stomach tightened as he realized they may have found the research floor. April had been on one of the observation floors, but never saw this area. Hardly anyone did. Grant had only been in there once and vowed never again. He could still turn back and disappear, but no point in that now.

As he turned the corner he was right. The rest of the center's staff was standing around just inside the research area, looking terrified. He knew he had to be careful not to get within April's line of sight so as not to fall under her spell. Carefully he crept in behind, a few of the staff saw him, he put his finger over his lips as if to say "shh!" As he worked around the back side of the group, he spotted April and the other girl standing inside staring at the headless body with the living head.

That was new. Last time he'd been up this way, there

was no dismembered head that could still talk. Though it was probably the least odd thing on this floor. Cassidy had told him they do various studies on the human body and nervous system. One thing they seem to enjoy is seeing under what degree of dismemberment and transformation the body and brain can continue to function. The whole thing seemed sick to him, but they claimed it was in the name of science and progress.

He wasn't even sure where they found these poor souls. Rumor had it they had a deal with the prison system. That wouldn't have surprised him in the least. Grant couldn't help but think that no matter what a person did, being experimented on like this wasn't something anyone deserved. None of that mattered at the moment. Nothing he could do to help these folks. But he could rescue the rest of this staff from April and her pal.

Slowly he raised his gun, zeroing in on the back of April's head. It was a dead shot at this distance. As he squeezed the trigger, her partner glanced at him, spun around and opened fire. He managed to dive out of the way, but the crazy bitch had no regard for any of the staff standing around. Several went down around him as blood showered him. Lying face down he low crawled down the hallway to the next room.

More gunshots splintered the doorway just as he ducked into the room and slammed the door shut. As he gathered himself, there was a groaning sound from behind him. There strapped to the bed was a man in some kind of bubble with a heater going next to it. Inside the bubble, the man had no flesh at all and very little muscle. Grant could see the man's heart beating between the exposed ribs and lungs breathing.

The man let out additional groans as Grant looked at him. He couldn't tell if the man was trying to communicate, or if he just in so much pain he couldn't not make noise. Grant shook his head as he nodded and looked back to the door. He heard the girls yelling at each other as one of them tried the door. More gunfire erupted as shots clanged against the heavy door, but nothing made it through the thick steel.

He could probably stay holed up in there as long as he wanted, but that wasn't the plan. Chances are they would fuck around with the door until they got in. They made it through the first set of doors. Sure enough in less than ten minutes someone was working the keypad just as the lock hissed and the door slowly opened. He kept his gun trained on the door waiting for the first sign of anyone.

A woman's head did appear around the corner and he fired. The bullet struck her square in the forehead as her body toppled to the ground. It wasn't either of his attackers. It was some poor staff girl. Chances are she had no idea she'd die at her job when she got hired. Something they wouldn't mention during orientation.

The door burst open and at least a dozen of the staffers came charging in. Grant shot, knowing April was controlling all of them. He fired several shots until his gun was empty. He'd taken down four or five of them, but they kept coming. Some were crying, others were yelling while others just had blank expressions. Either way, he stood and began fighting them off, but they got him off balance, got him to the ground and piled onto him. He struggled but all these folks on him were either super heavy or really strong.

More footsteps sounded as he looked up to see April and her friend,

"My name is Isis, asshole," the girl said. Now that was bizarre.

April and Isis were staring down at him.

"Thanks for giving me that head start," she said.

"Yeah. You owe me one."

"Maybe. I want to take control of your brain so badly, and make you do some really awful things to yourself. Problem is, I have to make you get off first. I hate to give you any sort of pleasure, but I might half to, at least let you feel one more good thing before all that suffering."

"Now why would you do that?"

"Are you fucking kidding me?"

"Can I just blow his nuts off? We can still torture him, hell you can let me do this one," Isis said.

"You know what. That's a good idea. Save his nuts though. We'll cut those off last."

"I like how you think girl!" Isis said as April had them pick him up. Isis kicked the heater and machines away from the bed and looked at the skinned man within the bubble.

"Jesus Christ," she said. "You see this shit?"

"I know. What other fucked up people you have up here?"

"I don't know. I never went up here. My job was in the field."

"Right. Rounding people like me up, or killing them. How honorable."

"Look, you think if you kill me you're safe? I'm a single little worker bee in this big nest," he said.

"Whatever, this place is fucking wrecked, everyone is dead, and these guys all will be soon."

"That's what I'm trying to tell you. You think this is their only place? Jericho Systems is everywhere and part of everything. They want me dead too thanks to you. They're pissed you got away the first time. They just ordered me Dallas for a meeting. I knew it was a trap. Figured I'd at least try and take you out before you hurt anyone else."

"See? Such a noble man," April scoffed.

"Listen. We don't have to keep killing each other or people around us. Your ability, or gift or whatever, its' really strong. I can tell. Your dad told me all about you. You're a sweet girl. Never hurt anyone, not until this came along. I—I think I can help you." He was totally making this up as he went, but meant what he was saying. No way could he go back to Jericho. Maybe they could help each other. There was no chance in hell she'd go for it, but he had to try.

For a minute, he thought she was considering his offer. Until she spoke.

"Isis, put that guy on the table out of his misery and move him. You guys strap Cowboy Bob here to the table. Let Isis have a little fun."

This time he didn't even try to struggle. There were too many of them and he was too tired. Now he just hoped he could change her mind, or that she killed him quickly.

Chapter 25

April figured out a way they could really fuck with this guy. She didn't trust him at all, but part of her wanted him to be on the outs with Jericho. After the past several days of all the death and violence, the chance for some answers and maybe even a break really appealed to her. With what she had in mind for Grant, there was no way he could lie to them. They stripped him to his underwear and strapped him to the table.

"Don't fuck him up too bad," April warned. "We may need him later. If I decide we don't, then you can go to town."

"Oh don't worry," Isis said. "My old man did lots of shit on me that hurt like hell but didn't leave marks."

"Well good. I think. Let's get started."

"You're making a big mistake," Grant said. "Did you know your dad is the one who called me? He sent me to get you."

"Now you're treading on dangerous ground asshole. So if I were you, I would tread lightly," April warned.

"Listen. I'm not lying to you. He knew you'd been gone too long and knew what you were capable of. He was worried for you. It wasn't his fault they were going to kill you though. But he made a deal."

"Shut up!"

"They were going to send him to Washington in exchange for you. He was going to be a deputy director. They told him you'd just be observed is all, not harmed," Grant insisted.

"Fuck him up," April said.

Isis smiled as she took a scalpel and began slicing the skin between his toes, not too deep, but deep enough to hurt. He grunted and tried to hold in a scream as she went from toe to toe making nice and slow incisions. Finally he let out a scream as Isis giggled.

"This kind of makes me hot," she said. "I never just tortured someone like this."

"You need serious help," April said.

"Right, miss make them cum with my brain."

April looked at him as his screams turned into moans as he struggled against the restraints as a bulge appeared in his shorts. He wiggled and grunted as he got closer to climax.

"Cut him again," April said.

Isis took the scalpel and jabbed it into the bottom of his foot, slowly poking the pointy end through his flesh. His moans again turned to screams as April continued to use her mind, bringing him close to climax. She backed down after a few cycles of the pain/pleasure treatment as Grant was trying to catch his breath.

"Pretty fucked up isn't it?" April said. "You feel so good, so close to climax, then pain! Extreme pain! Then pleasure. I bet your body and mind don't know what to do."

"You're further gone than anyone thought April. If you want to kill me, just kill me. I told you we can help each other. I know a lot about Jericho, more than they think I know. If I helped you two, we could bring them down for sure."

"Just seems odd to me that you'd turn on them so quickly."

"They have a zero tolerance rule on mistakes. I finally made one."

"That you did," April looked at Isis. "Go back to work."

Isis started once again on his feet while April worked him back and forth on the brink of climax again. They did this for over an hour until April was satisfied Grant was telling her everything he knew. She finally let him climax as she took control of his mind and let him up.

"Now get dressed. You can live for now, but under my control," April said.

"That's not what I had in mind," he said as he tended to his bloody feet, wrapping them in gauze before getting dressed.

"I am what is in your mind, whether you like it or not. Now get dressed and let's go."

Gunshots rang out as April spun around. Isis had the MP-5 on full auto and was mowing down the rest of the Jericho staff. She then went door to door and room to room, killing whatever abominations may have been lying beyond those doors. April was glad she didn't have to see them at least.

"Jesus Christ. You didn't have to kill all these people!" Grant said.

"They were guilty, just like you. Look at this place. All of them were a part of it. So you are going to help me bring Jericho down for good. And how many like me are out there?"

"That we've located? Several dozen at least. Most are hard to find anymore. They keep a low profile and keep moving. You, for some reason can't seem to help yourself."

"Yeah thanks. Let's go."

They made their way out of the building and just down the street to where Grant was parked.

"Where we going?" Grant asked.

They wanted to see you in Dallas. So we're going to Dallas," April answered.

"They're going to kill me."

"No they're not. Let's go."

They drove north and out of San Antonio. No one had said much as Isis had even fallen asleep in the backseat. April jumped when Grant's phone rang. She let him answer it and tried to listen to his half the conversation, but he didn't say much. Finally he hung up and looked at her.

"Mind going back to Happytown?"

"Are you kidding me? For what?"

"When you trashed that Funhouse, apparently a couple of clowns escaped. They just wiped out an entire circus in a nearby town and aren't near done. Jericho has known about them for a long time, but for some reason just lets them do their thing. They'd like me to nab one and bring it in for them to study. Apparently they're not human."

"No they're not and the answer is no. I barely survived those fucking clowns, I'm not going near them again."

"We could just kill them, don't need to take it back to Jericho."

"Wait a minute. You just gave me an idea," April said. "Head toward Happytown. This will really be fun."

About the Author

Tim began writing at a very young age. Even in grade school he'd sit around with his notebook, writing stories for himself and his friends.

As an adult, Tim's writings have evolved into darker realms. He released his first horror novel, "The Hand of God" in 2011. Since then his books have become progressively more violent and gory. With the release of "Family Night" in 2013, Tim had moved into the world of extreme horror where he continues to push the boundaries of human suffering.

Tim is now an international best seller as well. His book, "Hell, Texas" has recently ranked high on Amazon sales charges since its release in Germany under German publisher, Festa-Verlag.

Tim is very active on social media and loves interacting with his readers. You can find him at his website at http://timmiller.org.

Also by Tim Miller

Series:

The Hand of God

Revenge of the Three

The White Devil (coming soon)

Dark Exorcist

Dark Exorcist 2

April Almighty Series:

Dead to Writes

Welcome to Happytown

Extreme Stand Alones:

Family Night

Hell, Texas

The Country Club

Bloody Bank Heist

Witches of Dark Rock

CPSIA information can be obtained at www.ICGtesting.com
Printed in the USA
LVOW10s1352080615

441616LV00001B/97/P

9 781508 533955